GARDENIAS AND A GRAVE MISTAKE

DIANA FLOWERS FLORICULTURE MYSTERIES

RUBY LOREN

BRITISH AUTHOR

Please note, this book is written in British English and contains British spellings.

A BAD BEGINNING

In under a year, I'd been to two weddings and a funeral. By the time June rolled around, and the third wedding loomed, I was feeling quite miserable. I knew that I was just at that time of life when my friends and acquaintances were all getting married, but for the first time ever, I was feeling a bit jealous.

I'd spent the latter part of my teenage years and the majority of my twenties focusing on a career in chemistry - specifically chemical analysis. During that time, I'd had one serious, long-term relationship. It had ended with a bang big enough to make it necessary for me to transfer laboratories away from the man I'd thought I was meant to be with. Several things had happened since then. I'd been transferred to a rural lab, that just so happened to be a few miles to the west of the village where I'd grown up. I'd moved back into the village, (renting an apartment after lasting all of a week staying with my mother) and I'd slowly started to realise I was in the wrong job.

It had begun with the allotment. When I'd rented the apartment, I'd been offered the outside space for a small extra fee. I'd said yes on a whim, but when I'd visited for the first time and had met my allotment neighbours and seen the interesting plants they were growing, something akin to an inner awakening had occurred. I'd governed my whole life logically for as long as I could remember. *Study hard at school, go to university and get a good degree that guarantees a job, work hard at that job and make a good living...* I'd done it all perfectly. It had only been after my relationship had gone so spectacularly south, and the world wasn't covered in roses anymore, that I'd been open to the idea that I might have missed something. That something had turned out to be flowers.

I knew that there were those in Merryfield village who found it amusing that my last name, which is Flowers, seemed to be telling me what to do all along. To them I would say that both my mother and father still used that last name and neither of them could grow so much as a stalk of cress, nor had any desire to. I was the family oddity.

I was also dangerously close to becoming the family outcast having handed in my notice at the laboratory in order to give my cut flower business a real go.

For my sister, Charlotte, this year had turned out to be her year. She'd been known as the wayward one when we'd been growing up, often being dragged out of pubs and clubs in the nearby town of Kingston Hill by our mother (much to the amusement of the locals). We'd never been the closest of sisters. Unfortunately, it was only now that I was starting to understand how my dedication to studying and attaining that 'Little-Miss-Normal' life had contributed to pushing her away.

The first wedding had been hers. She'd married a Londoner who worked trading Forex. According to my sister, it wasn't the kind of job you loved, but he would probably be able to retire at fifty. Then they'd live the rest of their lives in relative comfort. When she'd told me that she'd followed it up by saying: 'You understand, I'm sure'. It had been another catalyst in my recent decision to change the direction of my life. With Charlotte's journalism career finally starting to land her some credit, she was starting to look like the sensible and reliable one in the family.

I didn't begrudge her it at all. In some ways, Charlotte had been right all along.

Her wedding had been way back in January. It had been the only time her now-husband, Garrett, had been able to book off work.

The second wedding had been for my childhood best friend, Heather. She had married the man she'd been dating practically since they were in primary school together. It had only taken them this long to get hitched because they'd been focusing on building their B&B business in the rambling farmhouse that Todd's parents had left to him after they'd emigrated to the South of France. Apparently it was the family tradition to pass on the farm whilst still living, in order to give the next generation a head-start in whatever they chose to pursue. I privately thought that some people had all the luck.

I'd been maid of honour back in May for that wedding, and it had been a beautiful occasion.

Prior to all of the weddings had been the funeral. A village man named Jim Holmes had met his end when he'd fallen into a hole and broken his neck. Jim had been my allotment neighbour. I'd done my best to figure out what had happened to him when the police had expressed their doubts that there had been any foul play involved in Jim's death.

The biggest surprise of all had come when I'd been told he'd left me his house and a chunk of money to go with it. Prior to that, I'd been pursuing my flower business on the village allotments the best I could with the limited space available. Jim's surprise bequest had included the fields surrounding a house in a hamlet, just outside Merryfield village. It was the perfect place to start a cut flower business and Jim Holmes had known it - although, I was certain he hadn't imagined he'd be passing it along quite so soon. All the same, I said a silent prayer of thanks to my unlikely benefactor every day.

I looked at myself in the age-spotted full length mirror and tried to smile. My pointed chin and high cheekbones somehow seemed to sneer that I wasn't fooling anyone. I relaxed my face again, back to its usual no-nonsense expression. People (mostly men) had often informed me (mostly unasked) that there was something intimidating about my mannerisms. I silently agreed with them and had always been grateful for the fact that I was not someone who looked approachable. As far as looks went, I was happy with my shoulder-length hair with its gentle wave at the bottom. My only vanity was that I tinted it red. Beyond that, I usually let what I saw in the mirror be. I had blue eyes, fairly dark eyebrows, a narrow, straight nose, and lips that didn't need rouge to tint that fashionable shade of pink. I certainly wasn't envious of my best friend Heather, who was beautiful in a fair, English rose kind of way, but whose open face meant she got all kinds of attention - both good and bad. I was happiest left alone.

"I wish you were invited," I muttered to the hairy brown dog lying on the bed behind me. He lifted a fuzzy ear when I addressed him but then lowered it again, giving me a tired snort as his response. Diggory was about as enthusiastic about this particular wedding as I was.

I looked back at my reflection in Jim Holmes' old mirror and wondered if it was obvious that I was trying too hard. I'd broken my 'minimal makeup only' rule and had gone to town on my face. My skin was already a lot more tanned than its usual milk-white - courtesy of my recent indoor to outdoor lifestyle change. It meant I didn't actually have any foundation or concealer to hand that matched my skin, but also fortunately, the weather and hard work seemed to have worked some magic on my skin. I currently had zero blemishes. I was twenty seven and had long since discovered that spots, albeit only a few, do indeed stick with you long beyond your teenage years.

I batted my pumped up eyelashes and asked myself what all of this was for. *It's armour,* I decided, before giving myself the final once over, saying goodbye to Diggory, and walking out of the door to go to the wedding of my childhood sweetheart.

Perhaps it's exaggerating to call him a childhood sweetheart, I considered when I stood outside the quaint Kingston Hill chapel. The bells were already ringing in celebration of the special day. I felt the same butterflies floating around in my stomach that I'd experienced as a teenager when I had been totally and utterly in love with Spencer Byrne.

Everyone from Merryfield and the surrounding villages had attended the local comprehensive school in Kingston Hill. That was where I'd first laid eyes on Spencer. He'd been in the year above me and was very popular with girls. I hadn't been particularly popular with anyone, but there had come a time around sixth form when I'd decided that I liked myself, so it didn't matter what others thought about it. Back then, it had been a surprise that this actually translated into people liking me a whole lot more. In between manically studying for my A levels, I'd finally bitten the bullet and had gone to ask Spencer out... only for him to ask first. We'd gone on a couple of dates but then the school year had ended. Spencer had left on a gap year travelling the world, which the last I'd heard had turned into several gap years. There had been times in the years that followed when I'd wondered what might have been, but finding what I'd thought was love at the chemistry laboratory had ended those thoughts.

Until now, anyway.

I sighed and joined the throng of people filing into the chapel ready for the service to start. *Francesca Steele. How on earth did Spencer end up with her?* I wondered as I sat down near the back, trying to be as unobtrusive as possible. I hadn't laid eyes on either the bride or the groom for years. The invitation had arrived at my mother's house and had come as a complete surprise. I still wasn't sure why I'd been invited - beyond Spencer somehow wanting to make amends. Although, if that were the case, it was a funny way to go about it.

The groom himself stepped out from the front row and stood at the altar, looking back in anticipation of his bride appearing.

He was still as gorgeous as ever, I noted, my heart sinking even lower. Why had I come? This was like volunteering for torture.

I'd already stalked Spencer on Facebook after the invitation had been passed on to me. He was apparently working as an entrepreneur. There would have been a time when I'd have turned my nose up at that vague and dreamy title, but now that I was giving the entrepreneurial thing a shot myself, I could hardly judge. *If he's getting married, he must be doing all right for himself,* I reasoned, thinking of my best friend and her husband, who had wanted to wait until they'd achieved their financial and business goals. *Maybe I'll be the same,* I thought, fantasising for a moment about a wedding to an entirely fictitious man.

I was still blinking the ridiculous imaginings away when the church doors opened and the organ started up. In front of the altar, Spencer's face lit up with a smile I remembered from a time when he'd looked that way at me. I tore my gaze away and watched the bride walk down the aisle in a cloud of white.

I did my best to stop my jaw from hanging open. Even half an acre of tulle and embroidery could not hide the fact that Francesca Steele was very, very pregnant.

They must have had to rush the wedding preparations. Social media had also revealed the relatively short period of time the pair had been in a relationship together. I hoped for Spencer's sake that there was more to it than the conservative need to hang around for the sake of a child. After all - I was a product of what happened when your parents tried to make that work. I remembered Francesca Steele being a popular, but not exactly pleasant, girl in the year below me. She'd also been several sandwiches short of a picnic, but perhaps motherhood would change her.

I resigned myself to listening to insipid vows and wished that I had never replied to the invitation. When the service ended, I couldn't get out of there fast enough. My congratulations to the bride and groom were so swift I wasn't certain they even realised who I was. I was in the car and driving back home through the summer sunshine before the photo taking had even begun, silently grateful that I was unlikely to bump into Spencer or his new wife.

If only I'd been thinking things through - like just what Spencer was doing getting married locally after all of these years away - I might have realised that I was categorically wrong about that assumption.

The sunshine streaming down on my house and the surrounding fields cheered me up, just the way I'd known it would. I may only be five miles away from the church where the man I'd once loved had just got married, but it felt like a world away. I was not going to get hung up on the past when I had a future to bring to life - in a very literal sense.

I parked up by the old stone cottage and reflected that it looked a good deal better than when I'd inherited it. Jim Holmes had mostly lived in a cottage he'd owned in Merryfield. I supposed it must have been because the house and land had got too much for him to manage in his old age. I still wondered why he hadn't just sold the place, given the premium he would have got for the property and land in the current housing environment, but whatever his reasoning, I was happy he'd kept it. After a hard autumn and winter's work, clearing the largest field of weeds, shrubs and various debris, I'd ploughed up the land, analysed the soil, and was currently reaping the benefits of the winter's work with a flowering field of nigella, cornflowers, aquilegia, and sweet peas with the promise of more to come.

When I'd grown frustrated with the tough land, I'd wrestled with the house itself. A power wash of the exterior and a patch up, using some of the money Jim had left me, had been enough to keep the property standing upright for a few more years. I always reassured myself that the stone cottage, which was over two hundred years old, had remained in one piece for all that time. It wasn't going to fall down now. However, I also knew that all things came to an end, and I would have been a fool if I hadn't called in the professionals to at least make sure the place wasn't going to crumble to dust. Any jobs that didn't need professional input I'd taken on myself and slowly, but surely, the old-fashioned and outdated cottage I'd been given was starting to become a home.

"Now I've just got to make all of this pay for itself," I said, allowing the breeze to carry away my words. Thanks to Jim's kindness, I didn't need to worry immediately, but having a good and profitable summer would see me through a tougher winter, when most of what I'd be able to sell would be evergreen foliage. It would also prove to those who'd doubted me and, most importantly, to myself, that I hadn't gone completely crazy and quit a career in chemistry for a folly in flowers.

At least my new business had already garnered some local interest - albeit, not all of it good. Everyone in the village knew about the local girl who'd quit a fancy job (that had surprisingly inspired envy) to grow and sell flowers on a local market stall. At least - that was the only place where they saw me selling my flowers. On the plus side, it had definitely led to pity sales, but it didn't do a lot for my pride. But I would have to put all that aside if I wanted to succeed. It was about working hard, working smart, and praying that mother nature and a healthy dose of luck were on my side.

It was going to be an interesting year.

"What on earth...?" I muttered, pushing open the door to the house and seeing the carnage within. My immediate thought was that Diggory had run wild whilst I'd been at the wedding. He was pretty skilled at getting himself into trouble, but since I'd adopted him, he'd turned into more of a loller than a destroyer. The broken window further contributed to my conclusion that this wasn't the work of my wayward dog.

I'd been burgled.

2

ALL THE WRONG REASONS

I threw the disarray a cursory glance before rushing upstairs to check that Diggory was okay. To my relief, he was still snoring on the bed in the same position I'd left him.

I frowned. "Some guard dog you are!" All the same, I was pleased he hadn't tangled with the intruder. Broken glass could be mended, things could be replaced, but the safety of the animals and people we care about is something precious.

I walked back downstairs and had a better look around. With the gift of hindsight, I wondered if I'd accidentally barged in on the robbery in progress, but upon my return downstairs, I was reassured that there was no one else in the house. I was willing to believe that animal instinct had told me that from the start. The broken glass was from one of the large windows that looked in on the lounge/diner. It was definitely big enough for someone to climb through. Why they had chosen to climb through, or break in at all, remained a mystery. As far as I could tell, nothing had been taken. I didn't own a TV but my laptop was still sitting in its case by the toaster, and other than the mess, everything was much as I'd left it. I would have to take a more careful look around once I'd reported the crime, but it was a real mystery.

"Surely not..." I muttered, looking out through the broken window.

A man was casually strolling across one of the fields I hadn't yet tamed. Could the house-breaker really be so blasé?

I've always been the kind of person to make logical decisions under pressure. In my old job, I'd been great at delivering when private analyses were needed on some seriously short notice. That was the reason why I didn't immediately call the police or grab a weapon. It was because my analysis of the stranger strolling through the field didn't fit with my ideas on the appearance of someone guilty of committing a crime a very short time ago.

"Hey! What are you doing on my land?" I shouted once I'd grabbed Diggory and we were outside making our way to intercept the stranger.

The man looked up and waved. "Good morning! Or is it afternoon? It's so easy to get carried away when you're on the right trail."

I felt the wind leave my sails a bit as I was met with such an unexpectedly amiable greeting. I used the time I was flummoxed to take in the trespasser.

He looked like he was in his early thirties. His dark brown hair was short at the sides but sort of bounced around the top of his head in a manner I was sure most men would endeavour to glue down using wax. Somehow, I knew that its bounce suited the man in front of me, who wore battered Timberland hiking boots, generic blue jeans, and a *Jurassic Park* t-shirt that I would hazard a guess was the original - not a faux-vintage reprint. His dark eyes screwed up at the edges when he smiled at me and there was something winsome about the way his mouth crooked up more at one side than the other.

"Are you aware that you're trespassing?" I asked, finding myself unsure how to deal with the situation, now that I was pretty sure this man wasn't my burglar and even more sure that he seemed far too sunny to have any ill intentions. "My dog could have attacked you, you know," I added, hoping to instil some kind of concern in him.

His smile was unshakable. "Oh, really?" He knelt down and looked at Diggory. The big brown lummox wandered over to him, his tail wagging merrily back and forth.

"Well, you never know," I said, defeated by Diggory's own sunny disposition. The trespasser and my guard dog would make quite a pair.

The man looked up in-between pats and ear ruffles. "I'm sorry for trespassing. I, ah… wasn't aware that there was a new owner. I heard on the grapevine that the old man who owned these fields didn't check on them with any great regularity. I thought I wouldn't be bothering anybody if I came and had a look around." He stood up and dusted the dog hair off his hands before extending one of them to me. "Fergus Robinson. I'm a special researcher."

I extended my own hand. "Diana Flowers, chemist," I said, reverting to my old job title automatically when faced with someone claiming to be a 'researcher'. I had a moment of self doubt, as I wondered whether I was simply afraid to tell strangers that I was in the cut flower business because I didn't think I'd be taken seriously. How was I going to succeed in business if that were the case? I decided I'd said 'chemist' because I was still suspicious of this stranger. I wanted him to think twice before trying to pull the wool over my eyes.

"That's great! You'll know what I'm talking about," he continued, completely unabashed. "I'm here trying to gather evidence. My sources tell me that there are rare chemicals and minerals, perhaps even some kind of organic matter, in the soil here. My hypothesis is that the concentration of these specific substances, combined with some electro-magnetic and ley line interference, are responsible for the raised incidents of violence and other altercations that have taken place in this neighbourhood over the past fifty years."

"You think that there's something in the soil that's making the people who live here go crazy?" I summarised.

"Potentially. Once you start looking into it, there is a fair amount of evidence that suggests something is up. I've been over police reports across the time period I mentioned and even before that. Something definitely happened fifty years ago that kicked it all off. I think it's to do with the soil."

I found myself thinking of my benefactor, Jim Holmes' cantankerous ways. I had already got to know a few of my neighbours, albeit, not very well. However, it wouldn't have surprised me a jot if Jim hadn't been the ideal neighbour when he'd lived at the property. All it took was one bad apple and the whole bunch could turn. "Have you considered there may be other factors at work?" I asked, blithely.

"I don't think it's a coincidence, if that's what you're asking. I don't believe in them. In my experience, strange occurrences like the ones I've backdated in this neighbour-hood are generally caused by something in the ground. It gets into the water, which is usually what sends people nuts. Although, if you were to grow vegetables or anything like that out here... well, I'm sure the effects would be much, much worse."

"I can assure you, Mr Robinson, that there is nothing wrong with the soil here. I tested it myself."

"But you don't know what to look for."

I resisted the urge to roll my eyes. After the day I'd had, I was not in the mood to have the validity of my own analysis called into question by a man who was calling himself a 'spe-cial researcher'. "Enlighten me."

"It's complicated," he began and then winced, probably realising that saying 'it's complicated' was not going to fly with a scientist. "I just mean… it's sort of a work in progress. What my associates and I are looking for isn't yet supported by mainstream science. These substances we expect to find are subtle and often difficult to correctly identify."

Nope, he wasn't doing himself any favours at all.

"The soil may look just fine, but it's rotten. Every piece of evidence is pointing towards that being the answer," he finished.

"My flowers are growing just fine. The soil is a standard heavy soil containing clay, as is the norm in this region of the country. Now that I've added topsoil, plant food, and fertilisers made to my own recipe, I've seen excellent growth. It's going to be a great flower season." I left 'and you aren't going to ruin it' unspoken.

Fergus shook his head. "You're just churning it up. This is not a good place for… flower growing?" He looked incredulous at the concept. "Mark my words. Something bad will come of this, and your flowers will be to blame."

I sighed, my patience wearing out. "I'm afraid that my house has just been broken into. I actually came out here because I thought you were the burglar. You didn't happen to see anyone, did you?" I would be darned if I didn't get something worthwhile out of this mind-numbing conversation.

"I didn't see anyone. I was looking at the ground," Fergus replied with another all-too reasonable smile.

That figured. Had I really been expecting my luck to change now?

"I must report it to the police. Do feel free to come back when you have some scientific evidence to support your hypothesis," I told him in scathing tones.

Fergus kept smiling. The man had the hide of a rhinoceros. "I'll drop by for tea if there are any updates.

Leave it with me. But, if you'll take my advice, give the green-fingered flower growing thing a rest. What's wrong with a bit of wild English countryside anyway?"

"Growing flowers is my business."

The man's smile vanished for an instant. "Oh. Well... that's unfortunate." His genuine concern bothered me for a moment, before I remembered that the man was completely loopy. He hadn't presented me with a shred of valid evidence for why there might be something wrong with the soil surrounding my property. I was far more inclined to trust my own analysis over his 'not recognised by science yet' claims. Facts were facts. I wasn't going to lose sleep - or business - over any invisible negative energy and mystery minerals that may or may not actually exist.

"It was nice to meet you, Diana. I'll see you soon!" With a cheery wave, he wandered back off across my wild fields in the direction of Samara's property. I silently wished him luck. Samara was the formidable business woman in charge of the local rag, and I'd heard that she hadn't got there by being nice. I doubted she'd take kindly to a trespasser wandering across her land raving about magical minerals and rotten soil.

I looked down at Diggory. "Some help you are! First you sleep through a break-in and then you greet the nutty trespasser. We need to have words about your training..."

Strictly speaking, Diggory didn't have any training at all. He'd been living rough when I'd rescued him. He was a smart dog who understood that he needed to go outside for bathroom breaks and generally not trash the house, but he also took liberties like jumping up on furniture he was banned from and now befriending criminals. We should probably enrol in some sort of puppy class. *Better late than never,* I thought to myself, realising that I could probably find the time to go. The major planting of the season was over, and although there was a lot of maintenance, care, and (of course!) selling to do, I could probably squeeze in something like an obedience class. It would be good to meet some new people. Some new, *normal* people, I mentally adjusted a second later.

It was with great reluctance that I called the Merryfield police station to report the break-in. Even though I was technically no longer living in the village, the hamlet of Little Larchley fell under its jurisdiction. And that meant under Detective Walter Miller's jurisdiction.

I still wasn't quite certain what Walter Miller's problem was with me. Some days, I told myself that it was probably because he felt threatened by me on some intellectual level. On less charitable days, I concluded that he was too dumb to even feel threatened. Mostly I assumed it was because of the 'thing' that had happened between Walter and my mother before I was born. In a small village, having flings that didn't work out could be a big problem... because you ended up having to face them every day for the rest of your life.

I didn't actually know the details of what exactly had gone wrong, but I had zero desire to find out. Talking about anything of a personal nature with my mother was my idea of a nightmare.

Whilst I waited for the 'someone' the police were sending over to have a look around and take a statement, I considered who might have wanted to break-in to my property. More importantly, why had they picked today?

I paced up and down in my living room, silently lamenting the mess before wondering if the insurance that Georgina Farley (the lawyer who'd been the executor for Jim Holmes' will) had suggested I sign up for would cover the damage and possibly allow me to pay for the new carpet I'd wanted to put down in this room. Silver linings and all that jazz...

Come to think of it, she'd been close to adamant that I should have insurance for the house and contents. At the time, I'd assumed she was just safety conscious. To tell the truth, I'd been reluctant to pay out for the policy. Jim had left me some money, but a lot of it had already been eaten up by paying for house repairs, some essential updates, and of course all of the supplies I'd needed to launch my flower business. Paying for insurance in an area of the country where nothing ever seemed to happen had seemed like a waste, but I'd gone along with Georgina's suggestion, mostly as a sign of respect for her professional opinion. Now it seemed she'd been right all along. I couldn't help but wonder if it was something more than a coincidence.

The timing of the break-in bothered me. I could be wrong, but I wouldn't have been shocked if it was someone who'd known I was attending a wedding today. I knew burglars were opportunists, but my house was pretty far off the beaten, and it had been in the middle of the day. I was definitely inclined to believe that my burglar had known I was going to be at that wedding.

Unfortunately, most of the village would have been chatting about who was attending the event for the past couple of weeks, so it didn't exactly narrow my pool of suspects.

The final question to ask was why? Why had someone broken into my house and left it in a mess, but without apparently taking anything? That was what troubled me most of all.

I was still thinking and getting nowhere when the doorbell rang and I discovered the police had arrived. Daniel Herald, Walter Miller's underling, stood on my doorstep. I was relieved to see that Walter himself clearly had other matters to attend to today. Or perhaps he just wasn't looking for a fight.

It didn't take long to explain the scene and for the police officer to take some photos and ask a few questions.

"I'm afraid we probably won't find anyone. There aren't any fingerprints left behind. No one's that stupid anymore. Even if there were, if the prints aren't in the database, it doesn't help us at all. Nothing was taken though?" he enquired before I could even ask what was to be done about all of this.

"Not that I can see," I reiterated. "I'll have a better look later, but I don't think there's anything of particular value in the house. My laptop was right over there and the burglar didn't take it. I really don't know why they broke in at all."

"Perhaps they heard you coming back up the drive and ran off before they could get anything," the police officer hypothesised.

I nodded, realising that it wasn't a half bad theory. "I did leave the wedding fairly early," I confessed. A potential burglar who'd known where I'd be would definitely have been caught out if they'd imagined I would be attending the reception. The ceremony itself had been all I'd been able to take.

"It might just have been kids. This house was empty for a long time. They might have broken in for a lark, before realising that the house wasn't as unoccupied as they thought. I'll put the feelers out." The police officer hesitated for a moment, rubbing his reddish facial hair. "Does anyone else have keys to the house? Just a thought. I was at this crime fighting conference the other week and they reckoned that the people closest to us are those most likely to commit crimes against us. Interesting, right?"

I inclined my head briefly. "No one has keys apart from me. My neighbours, Alice and Tom, have a set for the storage shed, but that's it." They'd been cutting the small lawn around the house for Jim whilst he'd been living elsewhere. The fields had been left fallow, but the lawn had been very well cared for. For that small mercy, I'd been grateful to them.

"No other family might have a set?" Daniel looked hopeful for a moment at the prospect of wrapping up a crime so easily.

"No, they weren't given anything of the sort," I said, thinking darkly of Jim's granddaughter, Nina. She'd destroyed my allotment when she'd found out that I had inherited. She'd been given the allotment and his cottage in the village, but she'd wanted everything. In the end, I'd dropped the charges against her on the understanding that she would never return to Merryfield or its surrounding satellite establishments. She'd been only too happy to agree to those terms. The cottage had since been sold and the allotment rented. I was grateful to Jim for his bequest, but I was glad to have seen the last of his surviving relatives. "The window was broken. I'm assuming that they got in that way."

"Probably," the police officer agreed. "I just like to cover all eventualities."

I shot the man a look of respect. Whenever I saw Daniel Herald, he tended to be standing in the shadow of Walter Miller, and Walter Miller's shadow was a dark place to be lurking. I'd tarred the officer with the same brush.

"Thank you for your time," I said, walking back towards the front door with him. "I'll clear up in here and let you know if anything was taken that I might have missed."

"Give the station a call anytime," the police officer replied, rubbing that reddish beard again. He looked thoughtfully at me for a second before adding: "And ask for me... maybe before you say who's calling."

Boy, could I read between the lines.

At least Daniel Herald was as aware as anyone of the inadequacies of his boss.

I turned back to the messed up room when the police officer was out of the door and driving back down my long drive. Having a tidy up had definitely not been on my to do list for today, but shattered glass and ripped up cushions weren't the kind of thing you could postpone until you were in a more virtuous mood.

I started by grabbing the dustpan and brush and sweeping up the shattered glass. Diggory had sloped off into my bedroom as soon as we'd arrived back from the field, so at least I didn't have to worry about him stepping in it. I would have to board the window up with something until I had time to call someone out to repair it. My biggest concern as I swept up was that this inconvenience was going to damage my preparations for my second wedding of the weekend, which took place tomorrow. I had a bigger ball of nerves in my stomach than I'd had for Spencer's wedding today, but it wasn't because of any past love history. Instead, my concerns were purely business related.

My neighbour to the back of the property, Laura, was getting married to her fiancé Ryan. As soon as I'd moved in to Jim Holmes' old house, and had immediately paid for and put up signs advertising my new business, Laura had popped over and introduced herself. After sharing a cup of tea and some small talk, she'd casually dropped into conversation that she needed a florist for her wedding and apparently absolutely no one local could accommodate her.

With hindsight, that strange claim should have set alarm bells ringing. I'd assumed that everyone was busy and I'd happily agreed to do her flowers, rejoicing in the business it would bring. It was only later that she casually let slip that she wanted gardenias. Lots of them. My heart had sunk a mile. Gardenias were tricky little plants. Although I thought I would probably be able to get them flowering in time, with a bit of added protection afforded by a polytunnel, there were so many other flowers she could have picked. I'd suggested several alternatives, letting her know that gardenias are hardly appropriate for flower arranging, as they're not renowned for having long stems. She'd replied that all she wanted was a few little vases for the tables, and some pushed into the bouquets. It was simple!

I hadn't even been in business that long, but I already resented that phrase. I was seriously considering including a clause in my contracts for any 'can you just…?' requests and adding fees accordingly.

It felt like only yesterday that we'd hammered out the finer details.

Wait.

It had been only yesterday when bride-to-be, Laura, had hammered on my door with another last minute request. This time, she'd wanted to add some greenery she'd seen on social media to the table arrangements. I'd forced myself to think of the money she would be paying me at the end of all of this and had shown her some possibilities. Even now, I kept looking out of the windows at the front of the house whenever I passed to see if she would march in again and throw all of my plans into disarray.

It was on one of these trips past the window, carrying the remnants of the shattered glass, that I first noticed the gouge marks on the floor. It was with some surprise that I knelt down and discovered that someone had jemmied up several planks of the old, hardwood floor. They'd done a fairly decent job returning things as they'd been, but there were definitely marks that hadn't been there when I'd moved in. I should know. I'd gone over the place with a fine-tooth comb, knowing that any major property issues I didn't spot now would only bite me later (and probably cost a lot more).

I pushed my fingernails into the gouge marks and found the board lifted up. The nails hadn't been returned. I raised the plank and looked underneath.

Nothing.

There was just a small void between the floor and the grimy whatever it was that lay beneath. Foundations? Dirt? I was no builder. I focused my eyes on the space, looking for any evidence that there had been something stored there prior to today. I couldn't see any sign of the thick dust even being disturbed by a groping hand, but all the same, I was pretty darn sure that someone had lifted up my floor.

But why? I wondered, completely baffled. Digging around beneath the floorboards was hardly something the average burglar did. They liked to grab the obvious items and split - unless they had prior knowledge of where something was. I was willing to bet that in this case, it had to be the latter. Whoever had broken into my house had been looking for something specific.

But what? I wondered, having zero clue about how to even begin looking for the answer to that question.

For some reason, my mind went back to the time I'd first visited the house with Georgina Farley, the lawyer who'd executed Jim Holmes' will. What was it she'd said? *"Anything inside it now belongs to you."* Then there'd been a hesitation - slight, but enough that with hindsight, I was starting to wonder if Georgina had known more about the property she was handing over than she'd let on.

In the end, I threw my hands up and decided to get on with my day. I'd cleared the worst of the mess and I was only too aware that tomorrow I had a wedding to do flowers for and a professional reputation to uphold. Laura and Ryan were locals and there would be a lot of villagers and others at the wedding. It was the perfect opportunity to show off my flower growing and arranging skills in the hopes of gaining new business. But, if I wasn't careful, it could also be the perfect disaster.

"Fail to prepare, prepare to fail," I muttered, seizing my trusty iPad organiser and walking out to hit the fields. I strongly believed that fresh was definitely best when it came to flowers. All of the flowers would be cut today, conditioned over night, and arranged early in the morning. All I had to do today was set up my flower pails and make my best picks. I'd been used to early starts for a while, having had to burn the candle at both ends when I'd been juggling growing flowers and a job working in a laboratory. However, I knew that I didn't tend to make my most logical decisions when I was still half-asleep, so setting it all up and preparing the flowers, whilst I was thinking straight, was my way of ensuring everything would be just perfect tomorrow.

Or at least - as perfect as it could be, as far as I was concerned. I had some pretty big reservations about what Laura's view would be. I silently said a little prayer that one of the other contractors would draw her attention, perhaps by dropping a tray of nibbles, or not being able to source miniature prawns. It would be nice to have a free pass for the day.

I had no idea how much I'd regret ever having had the thought.

"Yoohoo!" a voice called when I was in the midst of my cornflowers, trying to figure out why the heck they'd decided to grow so tall. The seed packet had claimed they'd grow to be fifty centimetres, but these monsters were closing the gap on two metres. It was basically a cornflower jungle that had the other annoying effect of swallowing up the roses and love-in-a-mist I'd planted in the middle of the rows on the assumption that they'd get enough light to flourish.

I stumbled out of the wild plants, slapping my legs as I felt things biting me. Wasn't that typical? Not only had the corn-flowers become giant, they were also housing flesh-eating critters.

"Yoohoo!" the voice called again. This time I was able to see the identity of the caller. Alice Jenkins peered over the hedge that separated our properties.

"Coming right over!" I shouted, always wanting to be friendly to neighbours and visitors. Well - the ones I'd invited anyway! I'd already noticed that people around here were a bit nervous about saying hello or wandering onto my land. I'd definitely got the impression that there was some long history I had no idea about. Knowing what Jim Holmes' character had been, I wasn't entirely surprised.

"I hope things are growing well for you?" Alice ventured, all smiles. She was in her mid-thirties, and although she was nicely spoken, there was a steel in her that I appreciated and respected. She commuted daily to London and never talked about her job. The village gossips had it that it was some boring bank job, but I had a strong suspicion that it was something more challenging than that. Something that required you to have a strong backbone.

I replied that things were doing very well indeed. Too well in the case of the monster cornflowers. Then we made some other small talk before Alice dropped in the reason that she'd stuck her head over the hedge.

"Tom and I are thinking of renting out our garage conversion again. It's on this side of our house. I don't think that there'll be any extra noise or trouble. We do our best to vet our tenants, but I wanted to ask your thoughts before going ahead."

"That's fine! I don't mind at all," I reassured her.

A look of relief flashed over Alice's face. For a moment, I wondered what financial change might have driven their need to rent a part of their property out, but I quelled the thought. It was none of my business.

"I've noticed you and your dog are quiet neighbours. I just want to be the same for you," she answered with another smile.

"You seem just perfect to me. I'm still grateful to you and Tom for keeping the lawn mown all of this time."

"Oh, it was nothing. Honestly, our motive wasn't entirely unselfish. There was a time we considered selling up. Having the front of next door's house look like a wilderness that might be broken into by squatters is hardly a good advertisement." She smiled again to show no hard feelings. At least, not towards me. When I'd first moved in, I'd wondered why I didn't recognise any of my new neighbours from Jim Holmes' funeral. The months spent living here and hearing snippets of this and that had given me a good impression of why that might have been the case.

"I'm sorry Jim was the way he was," I said in the interests of bettering my own neighbourhood relationships. My benefactor was dead and buried, so I didn't feel like much of a traitor. Even I'd been able to find fault in Jim, and I was sure that if I'd picked vegetables instead of flowers and had dared to compete against him on the allotments he wouldn't have been so friendly.

"Oh, he was never too much of a bother to us. Even before he swanned off to the village and left the house here to rot we used to do his lawn. It's just good neighbourly manners, isn't it?" Alice shrugged like it was no big deal. "Anyway, Tom can do with the exercise. He spends so much time cooped up writing his books. It's not healthy." She sighed. "Of course, I'm usually the one who ends up doing the mowing, but anyway…" she trailed off, a trifle embarrassed about having shared so much about her family's inner workings. "If you ever need any help with all of this, we would be happy to come over and muck in. We country folk should stick together."

"That's very kind of you," I said, knowing that I wouldn't be so presumptuous as to take her up on her offer - at least not without offering some sort of financial compensation... and financial compensation was not something I had a whole lot of. "You know, I still haven't really got to know our other neighbours. I know Laura fairly well. I'm doing the flowers for her wedding tomorrow," I confided. "Other than that, everyone seems to keep to themselves."

"Oh, you know how it is! Merryfield folk have always kept to themselves. Those out here in Little Larchley are even slower to accept newcomers, I'm afraid. Sticks-in-the-mud, the lot of them! I suppose I think differently, working in London and all that. It gives you an appreciation for the benefits of living in a small community where you can actually get to know people. Those who stay here all the time don't have that. Anyway, you'll get to know them soon enough. Then you may regret your wish," Alice shared with a devilish smile. "They're not that bad," she hastily amended. "I know Jim rubbed a few up the wrong way, but I'm sure no one will hold it against you. Jim was actually always okay with us, but he did used to argue with Samara over there and then Jay over there..." she pointed in the opposite direction. "And you should have heard him shouting at Laura and her shouting back. It was so loud, I bet most of Sussex heard." She cleared her throat. "I can't say that I entirely fault his judgement in that case, but, well..." she looked embarrassed again for a second having spoken ill of a neighbour.

I picked my words carefully. "I'm working for her."

Understanding flashed across Alice's eyes. I knew I'd said

enough without saying anything actually incriminating, should it be repeated.

"Oh gosh! I forgot the main reason I came here. I think someone's been digging on your land? There's a pretty big hole just on the other side of our garden hedge further down the bottom. I haven't seen you in that field all that much, so I wasn't sure if you knew about it, but it definitely wasn't there a couple of days ago. I noticed it on my way over here." That was Alice's tactful way of saying the field next to her house was still as wild as the day I'd bought the property. Unfortunately, it was the truth. I had limited spending and manpower and had realised that focusing on one field first was the best way to start bringing in money sooner. Then, and only then, would I have the time and money to transform the other fields into my flower farm.

"It's probably my dog, Diggory. He has a bit of a track record for digging holes."

Alice shrugged and looked a bit troubled. "Possibly, but it looked to me like a spade might have been used." She looked up from under her eyelashes at me. "You know, sharp edges and that. But I'm no expert."

"I'll have a look," I assured her, my thoughts returning to the trespasser I'd seen off my land earlier in the day. He hadn't been carrying a spade, but what if it wasn't the first time he'd been on my land? "I was broken into today," I said, scarcely able to believe I'd forgotten to mention it up until now. I'd been so busy focusing on the wedding tomorrow (and, if I were being truly honest, moping about the wedding I'd been to that morning) the events of the early afternoon had flown from my head.

"Broken into? What?!" Alice said, looking more alarmed than I'd felt when I'd discovered the damage.

"They broke my lounge window to get in but didn't take

anything. I called the police and Daniel Herald came and investigated. But it's strange..."

Alice was frowning. "What kind of burglar breaks in but doesn't take anything?"

"Beats me," I said, with what I hoped was a reassuring smile. "We should probably spread the word to be on alert." See? I could be a good neighbour!

"I'll be sure to. By the time we all shuffle along to Laura's big wedding tomorrow, everyone will know," she assured me. "Unless Laura bans people from talking about it in case it detracts from her." Alice rolled her eyes. She wasn't above letting her feelings be known. I responded with a careful smile, only too aware of my precarious position as Laura's current employee.

Alice sighed and looked off towards the distant green hills of The Downs. "As if this wedding hasn't been divisive enough already... Laura's been rubbing it in everyone's faces for months. I just worry about Jay." She shook her head and looked at me before realising that I wasn't following. "His fiancée left him right before his wedding. As far as I know, he hasn't even heard a whisper from her since. Can you believe that? Some people are terrible!" We shared a moment of silent appreciation for what the world had become. "Anyway, I think anything 'wedding' is tough for him. Still... it will all be done and dusted tomorrow. Then we can all move on with our lives."

I nodded, perhaps a little more enthusiastically than I should have done. "Back to our sleepy village life, hmm?"

But tomorrow's wedding wasn't going to be one that anyone would forget easily.

And for all of the wrong reasons.

3

CAKE CALAMITY

The first thing I did the next morning was to look out of the window. The sky was clear, apart from a couple of cotton puff clouds, and there was that gentle pink haze in the sky that hinted it was going to be a glorious early summer's day. I breathed a sigh of relief. That was one weight off my mind. A beautiful day always helped create good moods, and I was nervous about this particular wedding. I had a strong feeling that the rug could be pulled from beneath my feet at any second, and I so badly needed this to work. This was my first big event.

"Come on, Diggory. It's flower arranging time!" I told the big dog. He lazily opened one amber eye and then shut it again. I gently rolled him off the bed. To my bemusement, he slumped right back down on the floor and went to sleep again.

"Breakfast!" I tried, recalibrating my approach. This proved to be more effective.

In what felt like no time at all, we were at the wedding venue. Laura and Ryan were getting married in a beautiful barn just outside of Merryfield that had been registered for civil ceremonies. I considered how lovely the rambling old building looked standing tall against the sky in the middle of a field of wild flowers. Marquees had already been erected around the outside, and I could only assume the caterers had done their setting up the previous evening. For just a second, I felt a pang of envy, before I quashed it. I should be thankful that I was out of my longterm relationship. My ex-boyfriend had shown his true colours and I was grateful that it had happened then, rather than much later. I had a life, and it was one I believed was infinitely better than the life I'd left behind.

With a determined smile, I started unloading my pails full of flowers and then the vases after that. I'd already made the bouquets and would deliver them immediately after I'd done my setting up here.

I glanced down at the short pail full of cut gardenias and said a silent prayer that everything would be okay. The gardenias had grown brilliantly and smelled amazing. Unfortunately, they were just as short as I'd known they would be and they certainly weren't what I'd consider to be a flashy flower - like a rose. If it had been anyone else getting married, I wouldn't have been so concerned, but I'd definitely gotten the impression that Laura wasn't an 'understated' sort of bride.

I pushed the thoughts from my head, giving my silent supporter, Diggory, a good head ruffle. Then I got busy creating the centrepieces for the tables in the barn.

"Drat!" I said when one of the vases tipped over and the absorbent beads I'd bought for the occasion scattered everywhere. At least they'd already sucked up most of the water, so the spillage wasn't too major.

I glanced at my watering can that I'd been topping up with the water in the flower pails and realised I needed to concede defeat and go in search of water. Nothing had stirred in the barn or the marquees since I'd arrived at the venue, so I could only assume that I was on my own. I figured that the catering tent probably wouldn't miss a bottle of water or two. I went in search, starting in the large marquee next to the barn.

The tent was filled with a makeshift kitchen that even had a giant stainless steel refrigerator plugged into a humming generator. I walked in that direction, noting the extensively stocked bar and wondering if I'd really quoted a high enough price for Laura Ripley. I decided I had. I'd already inflated it when I'd sensed that she might be a tricky customer, and I felt fairly compensated for my time and trouble.

Unfortunately, the bar was only stocked with alcohol, which would hardly have done my delicate flowers any favours. Sometimes a good shot of vodka helped to perk up a rose, but I was pretty certain it would be too much for sweet peas, cornflowers, and nigella. The gardenias would turn up their dainty toes given any excuse...

I moved past the bar, hoping that there might be a water tank set up. Surely there had to be a cleaning station? Catering was strict on things like that. I pushed open the set of flaps that divided one half of the marquee from the other and felt a cool artificial breeze on my face.

"Oh," I said, feeling all of the breath leave my body for a moment.

This half of the marquee contained the impressive multi-tiered wedding cake that was to be the pièce de résistance at today's nuptials. But it wasn't the cake that had taken my breath away. It was the man embedded right in the middle of it, having taken out half of the tiers and the icing in the process. He wasn't moving.

I took a deep breath to steady myself. I knew from my work as a chemist that shock releases adrenaline into the bloodstream. I wanted to keep a clear and logical mind.

I walked over to the ruined cake and the alarmingly unmoving man. Doing my best to avoid the mess of icing, I gingerly felt for a pulse.

There was no sign of life.

"Well, darn it all," I muttered. I'd wished for a convenient distraction for the picky bride, hadn't I? And now I'd got it. There was a corpse in the middle of the cake.

I bit my lip and took another deep breath, glad I'd left Diggory in the barn. He'd have dived headfirst into the cake, body or no body, with his appetite for things he wasn't allowed to eat. Whilst I felt my thoughts calm, I took in the scene.

When I'd walked into the air conditioned tent, it had been the cake that had drawn my attention. Once a towering work of patisserie art, layers of chocolate sponge, fruitcake, lemon polenta, carrot cake, and even raspberry ripple, now mingled with one another, mixed with cream cheese frosting, royal icing, and marzipan. The scent of almonds lingered in the air. Laura had certainly wanted it all when it came to cake.

Then I'd focused on the man in the midst of the destruction. Now that I looked again, I realised he was dressed in a charcoal grey suit. I racked my brain but couldn't remember finding out anything about what the wedding party were wearing. Even so, I was convinced that he must be a part of the event. He was dressed smartly. Or at least - he had been, until his outfit had been irreparably ruined by the mixture of cake and icing.

I shook my head. A man was dead. I shouldn't be thinking about fashion!

My eyes moved away from the man and onto the grass beside the cake, giving myself time to focus. A strange circle of burnt grass caught my attention. A cigarette had been dropped whilst still alight and no one had bothered to stub it out. It had burned for a bit, singeing the grass, but we'd been fortunate in that the weather had been decidedly British these past few weeks. The ground was still fairly sodden and so nothing had come of the small blaze.

Call the police! the logical part of my brain urged. I wasted one moment more, wondering just how furious Laura Ripley would be when she found out what had happened to her 'wow' moment. Then I dialled the number for the emergency services.

To my surprise, the first car to pull up in the dusty car park beyond the barn wasn't the police. It was with no little horror that I watched the bride-to-be step out of her silver Mercedes-Benz.

"Morning, Diana! I got up too early and have an hour to kill before hair and makeup and the bridesmaids all descend. I thought I'd pop up and check that everything is going okay," she called when she saw me. Everything about Laura's voice was cheery, but I knew from experience that it could change in an instant. I should have known that the overzealous bride wouldn't be content to just let me get on with it.

"I'm afraid there's been an accident," I said, for want of a better way to tell the bride that there was a body in her wedding cake.

The smile vanished from Laura's face. "An accident?" she repeated, the first signs of a fire of fury already lighting up behind her eyes. *Oh boy.*

"Someone has died. I found him in the catering tent," I explained, figuring that there was no better way to say it.

"What?! Who is it? How did they die?" Laura looked more confused than alarmed.

"I'm not sure. He's lying face down in the wedding cake," I added without thinking.

Laura's face turned ashen. "The cake? Someone's ruined my cake?"

I nodded silently, not failing to notice that this was the first thing I'd said that had finally caused some alarm.

Before I could do anything to stop her, she marched past me, heading in the direction of the tent.

"I don't think you should go in there! It's not nice," I started to say, knowing that it was the bride's wedding day and having the image of a dead body ingrained in your mind was not something I would wish on anyone.

I should have remembered that Laura had different priorities.

"That rat! He's really gone and done it this time. I'm going to kill Ryan!" she said as soon as she arrived in the room which contained the cake and the dead man. For one horrible moment I thought that the man in the cake was her husband-to-be. I hadn't been able to see his face beneath all of the icing and cake. Frankly, I hadn't wanted to look too closely.

"I told Ryan he should never have asked Troy-flipping-Wayland to be his best man. He's always been trouble, and now look what he's gone and done." She gestured to the ruined cake.

We both paused to take in the tragic scene again.

Laura's hand went to her mouth and she bit her nails before slapping the hand back down, remembering it was her wedding day. "Do you think we can clear all of this up? I don't want there to be any fuss…"

I looked sideways at Laura and discovered she was serious. "I've already called the police."

Her pout was immediate. "Why? They're going to ruin everything! It's obvious that he was being a disgusting, selfish pig and suffocated himself with his gluttony. He was probably drunk and thought it would be funny to destroy my big day. This just serves him right," she finished, just as Merryfield's finest walked into the tent.

"What seems to be the problem?" Detective Walter Miller asked, using his mouth but not his eyes.

I pointed in the direction of the man embedded in cake.

"It appears we have a sticky situation on our hands," the detective said, giving the hapless Daniel Herald a nudge in the ribs, as if his tasteless joke would otherwise be missed.

"He's dead," I said, hoping to instil some sense of the gloomy situation in at least one person present.

"I can see that, Diana," Walter said, ever the superior. "But what a way to go." He grinned and patted his own not-small belly.

I tried to resist the urge to roll my eyes.

"Will this affect my wedding? I've got guests arriving in three hours. Can't you just, you know... clean it up?" Laura asked, flapping her hands at the offending mess.

"Miss Ripley... police work isn't as simple as that. We must investigate thoroughly." Walter was in his stride now. "Do we know the identity of the deceased?"

"Troy Wayland," Laura announced. "He probably got drunk, took a dive in the cake, and was sucked under by the density of that lemon polenta. It's such a tragic waste..."

She was talking about the cake.

"I don't know... if you cut around the edge, I reckon you could still save some of it," Walter supplied, ever the professional.

"Aren't you supposed to be investigating? We don't know what he actually died of," I reminded him.

Walter's beady little eyes fixed on me. "It's Troy Wayland. He's been nothing but trouble since he was a kid, living in Kingston Hill. I used to hear about his antics from the station there. When he finally moved closer to London, I know a lot of people locally breathed a sigh of relief. If I were a betting man, I'd have told you that this was a forgone conclusion years ago. It was just a matter of when and how."

"A bad track record doesn't mean there couldn't have been something more at play here. How many drunken wedding cake deaths have you experienced?" I tried, unsatisfied with the way that this was going. I looked across at Daniel Herald, but he was back to studiously avoiding my gaze. No backup there then.

"There's a first for everything. Trust me, if I could pick anyone most likely to meet his end this way, it would have been…"

"…Troy Wayland," I finished for the detective. I was getting the picture. Troy had been a liability when he'd been alive and everyone was all too willing to assume that his luck had finally ran out, as it had clearly one day been expected to.

"Don't you worry, Miss Ripley. I'll call in for some help from the Kingston Hill lot. We'll be out of your hair and cleared up in no time. It may take a little longer than three hours, but we'll restrict our movements as much as possible to this tent. You'll hardly notice us, I promise," Walter was saying, all charm and smiles. That seemed to be the way the detective behaved towards anyone who wasn't me - especially when they disagreed with me.

I wrinkled my nose, starting to get bothered by the smell of almonds mingled with mushed up cake and sugar. I glanced down at the cigarette on the floor and wondered why the man hadn't put it out before diving headfirst into the cake. How drunk had he been to not think of doing that first? It was basically a reflex for chain smokers. Even though the cigarette was burnt, I could tell that there'd been a lot of it left when it had been thrown to the ground.

"I'm going to be late for hair and makeup. This is a disaster!" Laura burst out, her eyes filling up with fire again.

She turned to me. "You can get me a wedding cake."

It wasn't a suggestion.

I looked from the bridezilla to the ruined cake and back again. This wasn't going to be easy,

"Sure. But this is my fee…" I found myself saying.

Laura muttered something rude about it being the least I could do considering, but I hadn't been the one to ruin her cake. We may be neighbours, but we were not, and never would be, best friends. I didn't mind her knowing it either.

"Fine. Whatever. Bill me." She waved a hand in my face. "The flowers had better be perfect though. "Are those little white things the gardenias? I thought they'd be bigger," she tacked on, wrinkling her hateful little nose.

I kept my 'I told you so' to myself. Instead, I bared my teeth into a smile and returned to finding water to finish my table arrangements. With a cake to magic up from nowhere, I was going to be pushed for time.

This wedding couldn't end soon enough.

4

NEWLY DEAD

I know it's prideful to consider oneself to be smart, but I've always been a quick thinker under pressure. As soon as I'd stuck the last gardenia stem into the florist's oasis on the top table, I was out of the barn, into my car, and on my way to the supermarket. I only stopped en route to ditch the bouquets at the bride's house. Once at the shop, I hit the cake aisle. I arrived at the checkout with my trolley looking like a six-year-old's dream. Triple chocolate cake, carrot cake, a sponge with brightly coloured icing in balloon shapes, a fruitcake, and a lemon drizzle loaf I was going to have to cut down to a more sensible (and round) size were all present. I'd also thrown in cream cheese, enough icing sugar to last most people a lifetime, butter, apricot jam, a cake board, and some ready roll icing. Wedding cake 2.0 was in progress.

When I arrived home, I yanked an ancient recipe book out of my little-used kitchen cupboard. My gran had been a baker, but it had definitely skipped... well... all of the generations that followed. My mum had palmed her old books off on both me and my sister but, to my knowledge, neither of us was planning to break out into baking anytime soon. Still... today it could be a lifesaver.

"Perfect!" I said when I flicked through the section on icing and found a cream cheese frosting recipe. I was delighted to discover that I'd guessed the ingredients correctly, but that didn't surprise me. While I wasn't remotely interested in baking, I could usually guess the ingredients of any food with a fair amount of accuracy. I liked to think it probably came from a lifetime spent studying chemistry. I understood the components that made up a final product.

However, I hadn't thought of everything. It was only when I attempted to assemble the cake, and things started to go very literally sideways, that I figured I must be missing something. A fair amount of swearing and flicking through other recipe books later and I had my answer. I apparently needed some sort of dowel rod to jam through the middle to support all of the cakes and stop them from just collapsing in on each other. There was also a fair chance that the small fruit cake I'd bought was so heavy that it might sink straight through the other less-dense layers and wind up on the bottom. After a moment's consideration, I decided to skip that layer entirely. I would have it for my tea. I'd probably deserve it.

Another hour of frantic whisking and rolling later (mingled with some YouTube tutorials when the ancient illustrations in the books failed me) and I had created something that looked like a fairly passable wedding cake.

The bottom layer was the balloon decorated party cake, which had been rewrapped in white roll on icing. The next layer up was the carrot cake, neatly frosted in white. Then came the chocolate, which had been scraped off and then covered in roll on, mixed with a dab of the cream cheese frosting on the inside, almost as an apology to the interfered-with cake within. Finally, the hacked about and pressed together lemon sponge finished off the top layer, also covered in the textured frosting. The over all effect was plain, but pretty.

It made me frown.

This was the kind of cake that I'd certainly be happy with if I were the one getting married, but Laura was definitely a bride who wanted 'extra'. After racking my brain and knowing I didn't have the skill for fancy piping or icing modelling (today's masterclass had been enough) I decided on a far more trendy option.

I hit the flower field in search of edible blooms.

As luck would have it, this area was something I was already exploring. However, that didn't change the fact that I thought it was perfectly ridiculous. Yes, it was fun and fancy to add flowers to salads, but why? I'd tried them and they didn't taste particularly great or otherwise. They didn't seem to add too much excitement, in my view. But people seemed to like taking photos of them when added to their food, so I always took some edible flowers to the farmers' market to sell, and they always sold out in record time.

I rushed out and gathered an armful of brightly coloured nasturtiums, geraniums, and cornflowers. Fortunately I'd grown a lot of the latter. Then, I tossed the flowers into a fresh pail of water, loaded the cake into my car with a lot more care, and set off back to the wedding venue. I drove so slowly on the corners that I was overtaken by a tractor.

I could hear the gentle thrum of a large group of people gathered inside the barn when I arrived. I observed that the wedding must be in full swing. As Walter Miller had predicted, the day would not be affected by the death of a man everyone had seemed to view as a pain in the neck. I spared a thought to wonder why, if that were the case, Ryan Fray had picked him to be his best man. Then I wondered what he'd done when he'd discovered his best man would not be able to do his duties. I'd shaken that from my head, realising I was being sucked into wedding oblivion along with the rest of them.

There was a small police presence going in and out of the marquee where the first cake had resided. I was pleased to see people dressed in white bodysuits. Walter Miller was nowhere to be seen, too, which probably meant there was some actual good police-work going on. I left them to it and continued into another tent, hoping I'd find somewhere suitable for the cake I'd thrown together.

Mrs Dovey from the bakery looked up from the tray of canapés she'd been dusting with cayenne pepper and smiled. "Diana! It's a pleasure to see you here. I heard you did the flowers?"

I nodded. "Among other things. Was the cake yours?" I asked, inclining my head gently in the direction of the abandoned tent.

Mrs Dovey shook her head. "No, dear. That kind of thing is far too fancy for a common baker like me. You know what Laura's like. She likes things to be just so." She lowered her eyes, probably not liking to speak ill of the bride on her big day. I could empathise with the challenge. "Anyway, this catering lark is a boon for me. Most of the village is fighting a war against carbs and that means my bottom line is suffering. No one's thinking about their diets at events like this, and they pay pretty well. It is too bad about the cake though. I heard it was going to be very impressive. Too bad about Troy Wayland as well," she added at the last moment, exchanging another of those knowing looks with me. It would appear that Troy was in next to no one's good books - despite allegedly not having graced the local area for a long time.

Mrs Dovey shook her head. "Imagine a wedding without a cake!"

"Well, not quite..." I said and then confessed to my morning's extra task. "If I hadn't been there, I think she'd probably have collared Daniel Herald and forced him to do the job. Laura wanted a cake and I was just the unlucky victim," I said, knowing that I was speaking to someone significantly more qualified to pull off a wedding cake at the drop of a hat.

Predictably, Mrs Dovey's eyebrows shot up. "I didn't have you down as a baker. Did you manage to do it? There's hardly been enough time for even a simple sponge to cool... I'd have told her exactly where to get off if she'd asked me!"

Laura would have known it, too, I silently thought, knowing it was why I'd been the one coerced into this. "Come and see for yourself," I said, wanting to get an honest first impression from someone who knew the business.

We trekked back down to the car with a trolley for the cake to be transported on.

I opened the boot and observed that the darn thing was mercifully still in one piece.

"I'm going to add some edible flowers before wheeling it into the barn. They should cover up the less than excellent bits," I explained, knowing that Mrs Dovey would not miss my various slip-ups.

"Would you look at that! I've certainly seen worse that people have paid an arm and a leg for. How did you do it?"

I took a moment to bask in the praise before I confessed all.

Mrs Dovey's face was a picture for a moment before she giggled. "You're telling me that Laura Ripley, who demanded crayfish instead of prawns, because apparently 'it's fancier', is going to be serving up supermarket birthday balloon cake on her wedding day?" She grinned. "That's tickled me pink that has."

I just smiled, satisfied that the baker had been impressed by what I'd accomplished. If Laura turned up her nose, I would be the one stomping my foot. I'd done well.

"I just hope she pays up at the end of all this," Mrs Dovey said, shooting me a curious sideways look.

I gritted my teeth and nodded. I was taking the same thing on trust alone. Villagers didn't tend to charge other villagers deposits. The theory was, we all knew where each other lived, and you wouldn't live it down if you had debts to pay. But being shunned over not paying and those who had to suffer not being paid were two different things. I knew that Laura and Ryan had a fancy house - fancier than mine - but there were a lot of signs that this wedding was extortionately expensive. I hoped that she had budgeted well and wasn't expecting us to wait forever to have our bills paid.

I was also all too aware that living in a nice house in a fancy neighbourhood - no matter what the man I'd caught trespassing on my land might claim - didn't mean you necessarily had money to burn. I was the perfect example of that.

I was laying the flowers all over the cake, covering up the bodged bits, when Daniel Herald walked into the makeshift catering tent.

"Mrs Dovey, you wouldn't happen to have anything for the guys to have, would you? They all came out here without packed lunches."

Mrs Dovey rolled her eyes to the heavens, but she was smiling. "I'm sure I can rustle something up. I always bring extra to wedding parties in case something goes wrong."

"Including a backup cake? That looks great!" Daniel said, thinking he was complimenting Mrs Dovey.

"Oh, that's all Diana's work. She'll be putting me out of

business in no time," the baker said, aiming a wink my way. She was going to keep my supermarket secret.

"Nice one!" Daniel said looking impressed. "Dunno about the flowers mind you."

"They're fashionable," I said, feeling much the same.

"The kettle's nearly boiled, Daniel. How are things going in the other tent?" Mrs Dovey asked, subtly extending feelers of curiosity.

I kept my smile to myself. The village baker loved to gossip, and she was a master of putting you at ease before weaselling out the information she wanted to know. MI5 had really missed a trick when it came to Mrs Dovey.

"Oh, the Kingston Hill lot are doing the bagging and tagging and all of that. I think it's been going well, but they sure are taking their time." He shook his head. "Detective Miller and I have been taking statements. I actually need to get yours, Diana."

I nodded my acquiescence.

"It's useful that everyone's here for the wedding. We've just been tapping people on the shoulder and getting them to pop out before asking them when they last saw the best man. It sure beats having to chase around various addresses to gather information."

"Has anything interesting cropped up?" Mrs Dovey accompanied the more prying question with the freshly brewed cup of tea that she slid towards him across the counter.

Daniel Herald looked hesitant. Mrs Dovey made a plate of biscuits materialise from nowhere and he opened up. "Nothing to write home about. No one particularly liked the deceased. We haven't been able to talk to the bride or groom yet, obviously, but we've heard that the only reason Ryan picked him to be best man is because of some childhood pact they had that he wanted to honour." Daniel shrugged.

"Maybe Ryan thought he'd settled down in the years he'd been working in the city. Unfortunately, that's not the case. Troy Wayland had a criminal record as long as my arm. Mostly drunk and disorderly stuff, but a couple of assault charges, too. All in all - not a nice guy, and not someone you'd want to trust with a couple of expensive rings on your wedding day. Fortunately, the groom must have figured that much. He hadn't handed over the rings prior to the big event. It's lucky, or we'd have had to fish them out of the cake."

Mrs Dovey nodded and smiled approvingly as Daniel dived into the plate of biscuits, the hunger of his colleagues conveniently forgotten. "Nothing at all suspicious about this death then?"

Daniel's eyes lifted from the homemade lemon puff he'd been about to bite into before he relaxed. Mrs Dovey was a well-known member of the Merryfield Murder Mystery Fans book club. As well as reading classic mysteries, they tended to see suspicious circumstances everywhere they looked.

"Well... the bridesmaid, Julie Yardley, was the last one seen with Troy. They were out in Kingston Hill together last night. However, according to Julie, half the village was also out on the town, including the bride." Daniel shook his head. "I don't think she got much beauty sleep."

Mrs Dovey sighed. "Whatever happened to tradition?" Her beady eyes fixed on Daniel again. "Anything else?" she prompted, magicking up an entire sandwich.

The police officer eyed it. "What flavour is it?"

"Crab salad. That was always your favourite, wasn't it?"

He nodded and I saw all of his professional resolve vanish. Mrs Dovey was an expert.

"I also heard that the bride herself had some kind of history with Troy Wayland. She didn't want him to be at the wedding at all because of it. You can imagine what she must have felt when Ryan said he'd be his best man. Especially as - again 'apparently' - Ryan himself has no idea..." Daniel finished.

I felt my own eyebrows raise. Now that was some gossip worth knowing.

"There's nothing to suggest the death itself is suspicious. It's honestly a stroke of luck for all involved. Apart from Troy, of course," Daniel said, frowning for a moment as he bit into his hard-won sandwich. "One of the ushers said that they heard Troy was a gambling addict these days, too. I dunno why anyone would have given him the responsibility..."

"It was because I wanted to help him out. Sometimes all people need is a little push in the right direction to get them back on track."

We all turned around to see Ryan Fray standing in the doorway of the tent.

Daniel Herald placed the sandwich back on the counter and looked as sorry for himself as a man can look. However, the groom just smiled around at us.

"How did the wedding go?" I asked, hoping to break the ice.

"Perfectly. I'm now a married man. Thanks for the flowers, they were perfect and they smelled amazing. I knew Laura made a good choice."

I smiled back at Ryan. He'd served as the voice of reason throughout most of my dealings with bridezilla. At times, I'd questioned how a man like him could put up with a diva like Laura, but I thought they must somehow balance one another out.

"That looks like a wedding cake..." the groom said, looking hopefully at the finished four tiers.

"It is," I confirmed.

"You really are a saint. Laura will love it," he said, which I took to mean that he would tell her to love it.

I smiled my thanks. It was good having a man like Ryan on my side.

"Hey, Ryan… the photographer is ready." A man poked his head into the tent.

"Fergus?" I said, astonished to recognise the trespasser from yesterday.

He grinned at me. "Nice to see you again."

Ryan looked from me to Fergus and then back again, clueless. "This is my best man. I've known Fergus since university. With hindsight, he should have been my best man all along. He's much more sensible and reliable."

"Really?" I couldn't help blurting.

Fergus raised his dark eyebrows and gave me a winning smile. "To be fair to Ryan, a lot has changed since university."

"Daniel!" Walter Miller stomped into the tent shouting.

The police officer guiltily shoved his sandwich behind his back. "Yessir?"

"We need to put the bride under arrest. It's murder and…" The detective trailed off when he noticed that the groom was standing right there, listening to all of this. Walter Miller cleared his throat. "I'm sorry, but the forensics believe that Troy Wayland didn't suffocate on the wedding cake. He was poisoned."

"The cake was poisoned? We could all be dead!" Ryan looked aghast.

Walter Miller frowned. "Actually, they're not sure what poisoned him. I, uh… don't think it was the cake." A look of extreme guilt and fear spread across the detective's face. I noticed for the first time that he had a greenish tinge about him. Well, well… Walter Miller had interfered with the evidence.

"Why are you arresting my wife?" Ryan looked justifiably angry.

"Well, it's uh… tricky." Walter Miller faltered. He hadn't intended to have to explain himself to the man who'd just got married. "Someone witnessed the bride, uh, kissing the best man last night. Then, the lot from Kingston Hill found a, uh, monogrammed personal item belonging to the bride to be in the deceased's possession. I'm sorry," he hastily added, fully aware that it would be devastating news to the man who'd just got married to an unfaithful woman.

Ryan looked tired for a full three seconds before he shrugged. "She probably had too much to drink again."

I thought my eyebrows were probably just about disappearing into my auburn hair. This wasn't Ryan Fray's first rodeo by any stretch. He'd already known that his wife wasn't completely loyal to him.

"Oh, Ryan… why marry her?" Mrs Dovey said what I wanted to say but couldn't. Her seniority made it possible.

The groom looked pained. "I love her. She's not that bad. She just makes bad decisions when she's had too much to drink. We're working on it…"

Walter Miller looked perplexed and then put out. "Well, uh, she looks to be a suspect, I'm afraid. We believe she might have had a fit of regret and killed Troy Wayland because he was going to interrupt the wedding. You know… like they do in the films. Speak now, or forever hold your peace…" For just a second, the detective's eyes grew misty and a smile appeared beneath his moustache. I silently revised my thoughts about Walter Miller's television preferences. It would appear that he was less of a gritty thriller type and more of a rom-com man. Wonders never cease.

"I think it's ridiculous," I said, surprising myself by saying it out loud.

Everyone stared. I realised I'd now have to justify my

surprising statement. "If Laura had wanted Troy Wayland dead, there is absolutely no way she would have ruined her wedding cake to do it." Of that I was completely certain. They hadn't been there when Laura had seen the ruination of her star of the show. Even if she'd been able to feign surprise at the man's death, the fury on her face when she'd witnessed the destruction wrought on her wedding cake was surely impossible to falsify.

"Well, that's that then. She must be innocent," Walter Miller sniped, acting like the fool I knew him to be.

"I am innocent, you moron!" Laura herself burst into the tent. I wondered how she'd discovered she was due to be arrested and then gave up wondering. The way gossip worked around here defied all logic and explanation.

"We have multiple statements placing you with the deceased yesterday evening…" Walter Miller began.

"Oh, that was just silliness. It wasn't anything serious! You know that, don't you darling?" she said, turning her doe eyes on her new husband.

He nodded, not looking entirely happy, but also not bursting into a fiery blaze of rage. I decided that if Ryan was so lacking in backbone, he did deserve a bride like Laura after all.

"Laura Ripley… I mean… Laura Fray," Detective Miller said, correcting himself. The bride preened and shot a simpering smile at her husband. "You're under arrest under suspicion of committing the murder of Troy Wayland," he finished wearily before nodding to Daniel that he should cuff her.

The police officer gave up hiding his sandwich behind his back and shoved the whole thing into his mouth. With his cheeks puffing out like a hamster, he clipped the metal bracelets onto Laura Fray's wrists.

Walter Miller shot him a look of disgust, but Daniel

Herald looked defiantly back. He was willing to risk disciplinary action for the sake of a crab salad sandwich. Mrs Dovey should be proud.

"It's the most exciting wedding I've ever been to. How about you?" Fergus Robinson sidled up to me as I was loading up a plate from the buffet. Technically, I hadn't actually been invited to the wedding, but with the bride under arrest and the gloomy prospect of potentially never receiving a penny for all of the work and effort I'd put in, I was going to get some kind of value out of this. Anyway - I'd totally earned it.

"It's definitely up there," I said, thinking bleakly of the wedding I'd attended just yesterday. Sure, no one had been murdered, but I'd felt like I was being punched in the gut.

Fergus looked curiously at me but clearly thought better of enquiring. "I am sorry for Ryan. Although, he doesn't seem to be taking it too badly, does he?" We both looked across at where the bridegroom was filling his plate and laughing along with other guests who'd come up to congratulate him.

"She'll be out in five minutes flat. Her dad went with her to the station. He's a lawyer who's managed to get some terrible people off their terrible crimes. Convincing local police to release an innocent woman will hardly cause him to break a sweat..." the groom was saying to everyone in earshot.

"Did you know that about Laura's dad?" I asked Fergus.

"Uh... yeah. Ryan's been with Laura since the end of university. 'Daddy's' got her out of some scrapes like this before. Well... not exactly like this. Not murder. But... you know Laura."

Unfortunately, I did.

"I wouldn't be surprised if she really did kill him," Fergus told me, as cheerily as someone announcing that they were going on holiday next week.

"Really?" I still stood by what I'd said to Walter Miller about the wedding cake. Laura would have picked a much tidier and less wedding-ruining way to kill Troy. And with her husband on a leash, she hardly needed to worry, anyway.

"Ooo yes. Or if not her, one of your neighbours. Your neighbourhood has a dark and murderous past. Just look at everything Laura's father has done for some really awful criminals. He grew up in the house she now lives in, you know." Fergus took a sip of his Prosecco before continuing. "I knew something like this was brewing. It's the reason why I was looking around the area. You never know what someone might have buried. Those minerals and the negative magnetic energy could have made them do it. It's all in the soil…"

I took a not so subtle step away from the crazy man.

Then I remembered some recent damage to my property and aligned it with what he'd just said.

"Hey! Have you been digging on my land?"

Fergus opened his mouth, no doubt with some implausible excuse. "Look! The bride is back," he said, nodding to the police car that had just pulled up. "I'd better go give some sort of a best man's speech. I doubt I'll do any worse than Troy Wayland would have managed," he said, dropping me a cheeky wink before sliding away from me and the trouble he'd been about to land in.

I made a mental note to find out more about Fergus Robinson. He seemed intent on digging around in the dirt around my house, but I wasn't convinced that he didn't have dirt of his own to hide.

And with Laura Fray off the hook, we were missing a murderer.

5

DIGGING UP THE TRUTH

I t was amazing how murder could bring a community together. I got to know my neighbours better in the days that followed the wedding than I had in the seven and a bit months I'd been residing at Jim Holmes' old house.

The day after all of the drama, I'd intended to take some 'me' time. It was one of the benefits of being officially self-employed. If I were being honest, I was usually far more guilty of working without any breaks whatsoever.

The prospect of a day off was making me itchy, so I'd decided to keep it productive by cleaning the house. Cleaning wasn't something I was particularly enamoured with, but it was almost like meditating. There were an awful lot of things you could think about whilst scrubbing the bathtub.

What I ended up musing about was a lot more mysterious than I'd anticipated. The more I cleaned out the nooks and crannies around the house, the more I realised that they'd been disturbed - and fairly recently, too. I wasn't exactly house proud, but I wasn't a slob either. If I wasn't much mistaken, I'd hazard a logical guess that the signs of disturbance had appeared during the time I'd been burgled. There were scratches in the back of the wardrobes. Carpets had been pried up and then placed back down. There were even gouges where someone had desperately tried to lever up the lid of the large oak trunk I'd had since I was a child and had taken to the house with me. That gave me a hint that the burglar, or burglars, hadn't known much about the inside of Jim Holmes' home prior to his death. However, that didn't do much to narrow the pool of suspects. I very much doubted that Jim had invited many people over for tea during the years he'd lived here.

I sat down on the trunk and thought.

Had the searcher found what they were looking for? I discovered I was inclined to think that they hadn't. It was something about the carelessness of leaving the gouge marks and then the loose floorboards. They'd been in a rush, and they'd had no idea where to start looking. Of course, I couldn't be certain that they hadn't found the item they were looking for, but I'd got to know Jim fairly well during our time spent together on the allotments. In fact, it was that pastime that made me suspect that, if he had hidden something, it wouldn't be in the house at all.

Jim had loved his vegetables. When the house here had presumably become too much for him to manage, he'd moved to a cottage in Merryfield and taken on an allotment, where he'd grown to his heart's content. A few remnants of his horticultural time spent here in Little Larchley remained. Two of these remnants had baffled me ever since I'd moved in. To the average onlooker, the terracotta urns that flanked the entrance to the workshop were a nice decorative touch. They each contained a sturdy little tea tree. I'd wondered what sort of plants the urns had contained when I'd moved in. Careful research, and some even more careful steaming, rolling, drying, and tasting, had driven me to the correct conclusion. I'd initially been surprised that they appeared to be growing so well. Tea was something exotic, right? But further research had revealed that only the Indian camellia sinensis assamica variety liked to be kept warm. Camellia sinensis sinensis was hardy and well-suited to being grown in Britain.

But the unusual nature of having a couple of tea trees wasn't what had struck me as strange. Instead, it was the fact that they were there at all - and planted in decorative urns, no less! Jim had once had an interest in growing flowers, but in later life, vegetables had become his sole and all consuming passion. Decoration and something frilly and exotic like a tea tree was not in the pumpkin-growing, marrow-farming man's nature. I'd concluded that the urns and their contents must have been a well-meaning gift from someone, but now… I was starting to wonder.

Putting my hypothesis to the test was another question entirely.

I walked outside into the June sunshine, doing my best to look like I wasn't up to anything in particular at all. Diggory pottered around at my heels and then dove off into the marigolds that grew by the long path that led along the fields and then out to the workshop. I suddenly remembered I was far more often seen working in the garden like a maniac. Acting casual was probably far more suspicious. I mentally threw my hands up in the air and then physically rolled my sleeves up, heading straight for the urns and grabbing a trowel along the way. They needed a good weed anyway and I was a gardener. Gardening was a normal thing for me to be doing.

All the same, I couldn't help looking over my shoulder across the surrounding fields and towards the distant over-looking houses of the hamlet. It was with no little annoyance that I realised Fergus Robinson and his crazy conspiracy theory had got under my skin.

I jabbed the trowel into the soil around the first tea tree. Then, I dug down a little deeper.

"Huh!" I said as my little digging implement struck something hard. Had I found something? I gently reached a hand down through the loose soil and tried to feel what I'd hit. It was with a frown that I realised I'd hit the bottom of the container. The urns may look big and fancy, but the bottom of the actual planter was pretty darn close to the top. Nothing could possibly be buried in it. I was actually surprised that the tea plants were looking as healthy as they were, considering they were pretty pot-bound.

I bit my lip and looked at the tubs. They weren't actually even made of terracotta. They were plastic treated to look like the real deal. I wrapped my arms around one and lifted it up. Lack of watering had done me some favours, as it popped right up into the air. I walked over to the other and did the same.

I felt something inside the tub bang off the inside.

A jolt of surprise rushed through me.

There was something in this planter, concealed beneath the shallow bottom the tree sat on. I replaced the planter on the floor and wiped the beads of sweat from my forehead. I was glad that the pair weren't made of real terracotta or bogged down by water, but hefting them about still wasn't a walk in the park. I also used the opportunity to check to see if anyone had been watching. I couldn't tell if behind a distant window pane there were observant eyes, but I didn't think I was doing anything too suspicious. The trees needed potting up... and I was going to drag them into the workshop in order to accomplish that.

Ten minutes later, both planters were inside and I'd shut the door - in spite of the warm weather. I had no idea what I was going to find in the one that had rattled. If someone had been desperate enough to break into my house to look for whatever it was, I would be a fool to discover the truth out in the open.

I lifted the tea tree out by its trunk. It came up easily, roots wrapped into the shape of the shallow planter. The tree was unceremoniously dumped into a chipped terracotta pot. I got on with the task of flipping over the whole darn urn.

Some puffing and panting later, it was upside down and I was contemplating the saw marks on the bottom of the pot, where someone (I could only assume Jim) had cut a hole and then glued the bottom back in place afterwards. My bene-factor may have been a whizz at persuading vegetables to grow, but he was no DIY expert. The cuts were jagged and one good jab with my trowel was enough to force the bottom in.

I pushed it to one side and looked into the urn, eager to discover what my burglar had been searching for.

It was a bag of human bones - enough to make an entire skeleton.

"Not quite," I muttered as I looked in at the sorry pile of parts and realised that there wasn't a head. I couldn't even be sure that it was a complete skeleton, as the yellow bones were jumbled up in a clear bag - the sort you might store sports gear in. However, my training as a chemist had occa-sionally brought me into contact with cadavers (when unknown substances implicit in the cause of death needed analysing) and I was familiar with human bone structure. I knew what I was looking at.

I shut my eyes.

What on earth was Jim Holmes doing with a skeleton in his planter?

More importantly... why was someone looking for it? I was certain that it had been these bones that the burglar had lifted floorboards and gouged wardrobes in order to find. Now I'd hit the jackpot.

I almost wished that the burglar had found the bones and I'd never been any the wiser. Now I had human remains to consider what to do with and the strong suspicion that they hadn't been dug up from just any old place.

"Diggory... I think we might have a murder on our hands," I told my lazing dog. He lifted an ear from his place on top of a pile of burlap sacks where he'd settled when I'd been dragging in the urns. "Now what?" I murmured, looking at the bones and finding no inspiration.

The knock on the workshop door nearly made me jump through the roof.

I placed a hand on my chest to still the palpitations. Then I panicked. I was standing in the middle of a workshop with an upside down urn with a cut out bottom and a big bag of bones on full view, lying just inside.

"Just a minute!" I called when I saw the handle rattle. I was grateful I'd had the presence of mind to lock the door.

Thinking quickly, I dragged the bag of bones out through the hole and tossed the lot into my ride-on lawnmower's empty grass tank. Then, I flipped the urn back over and walked over to the door, hoping I didn't look like someone caught in the act of hiding a headless skeleton.

I opened the workshop door with a smile. "Sorry about that! I'm not sure why I locked the door, but I was up to my elbows in potting compost. I suppose it must be a habit I picked up in London," I explained to the knocker with a shrug. I knew it was an excuse that would go over easy with any villager. Their disdain for city folk's habits coloured their opinions.

"I knew it was something like that," the man at the door said, glancing down at my soil stained hands. At least my alibi looked accurate. "I'm Jay Donahue. I live somewhere to the right of you," he said, waving his hand in the general direction of some of my fields. "I saw you at the wedding and when someone told me who you were, I realised I've committed an unforgivable sin. You've been living here for months and I never introduced myself to you. I think we've waved at each other when passing cars in the lane, but that's it. It's not very neighbourly of me, is it?"

"I'm just as guilty. I never knocked on your door," I said with an answering self-deprecating smile. Next, we'd start apologising to one another, just to try and out-British one another.

"Well, I'm here now to say hello…"

"Pleased to meet you. Diana Flowers," I said, extending my hand and mentioning my name to save him the embarrassment if he'd forgotten it since the wedding.

He shook my hand and smiled. I realised that close up my neighbour Jay wasn't a bad looking guy. He had lightly tanned skin and creases around the edge of his eyes. There was something happy-go-lucky about him and the checked shirt he wore reminded me of the cheerful men on the back of cereal packets, strolling through fields of wheat with their equally ecstatic families.

What did I know about him? Alice had said that his fiancé had run off right before their wedding and had left him quite literally holding the baby.

"I actually came here to ask you something," my neighbour said, looking a little bashful.

I kept my eyebrows still and for once they behaved. "Oh?"

"My daughter, Lena, is going to turn ten this Saturday. She's quite grownup and I think it would be wonderful if she received a bunch of flowers for her birthday. I know it's late notice, but I was wondering if you might be able to help? She's having a party on the day, and I think her friends would be dead impressed if they were delivered during the event. Perhaps they'll even be the subject of envy." Jay winked at me and I found myself smiling back. It could be good for business. "You'd be welcome to stay for jelly and ice-cream afterwards. Goodness knows there'll be enough of it to go round." He shook his head and dramatically looked to the sky. "Why did I let a ten year old do the shopping for her own party?" He looked back at me, deadpan. "I think I'll still be working my way through packs of jelly cubes when she's all grown up and left home. And our freezer looks like a kid's dream…"

"I can do you a lovely bouquet for £20," I said, pricing it fairly, but a little kindly. I thought I'd struck a pretty good balance. "Do you know her favourite colours?"

We had a little chat about that and I made some notes in a notebook I'd forgotten I'd left on the work surface in the workshop.

"I'll deliver the flowers at 3pm. Things should be in full-swing by then, I'm betting? I'd love to stay afterwards," I said, a little cautiously. I wasn't sure if this was some kind of trap. I'd steered clear of men since my last disastrous relationship, and I wasn't sure I wanted to try again just yet. I had a business to focus on.

But then, I wasn't even sure if this invitation was anything beyond friendliness. Especially when Jay smiled and nodded like it was no big deal. "All right! See you then. I'll drop the cash through your door in an envelope, okay?"

I expressed that this was fine and then assumed he'd probably excuse himself.

He didn't.

"Listen… did you know that guy who died at Laura and Ryan's wedding? I can't believe they pulled each and every one of us in for questioning!"

I frowned. "Questioning? I thought they were just asking

for statements." I'd given my own and had been released without further trouble.

Jay shrugged. "Yeah, same thing, right? I hope they don't think I had anything to do with it. Obviously, I knew Troy Wayland by reputation. But who around here wouldn't know that?" He looked hopefully at me.

I grudgingly nodded. Troy had been a little my junior, but that didn't mean I wasn't fully aware of what a thorn in everyone's sides he'd been. I'd attended secondary school at the same time as him. My seniority had offered some protection. I'd been well-versed in the snappy retorts needed to defend my intellectual capabilities, but that didn't mean I hadn't detested the idiot boy.

"The police don't seem to be doing anything. I know Laura got arrested, but they wouldn't have let her go if they didn't think she was innocent…" Jay continued, undiscouraged by my lack of reaction. I silently thought that it was more that Detective Miller had failed to look before he'd leapt - given the wobbly evidence and the reputation of Laura's father. He should have known better.

"I'm sure they're working on the case," I said, neutrally.

"Who do you think killed him?" I knew it was the question Jay had been wanting to ask me all along - probably more than he'd wanted to ask about the bouquet for his little girl.

I sucked air in through my teeth, looking off to the distance as I formulated my response. "It might not be anyone we know. Troy hasn't lived in this area for a long time. He had a knack for getting into trouble when he lived in these parts, and I'm sure it's likely that he didn't change his spots when he moved away. But his troubles may have followed him back here."

Jay nodded but I could tell he was disappointed. He'd wanted me to point the finger at someone at the wedding.

"Who do you think did it?" I asked, surprising myself with the vapid question.

Jay ran a hand through his brown, shiny hair that was just aching to bounce up and down whilst he ran through the middle of a wheat field...

Wow.

I really needed to get out more if cereal boxes were starting to get me all hot and bothered.

"I don't like to speak ill of our neighbours..." he said, prefacing the ill-speaking he was about to do. "But... I think they should be looking more closely at whatever Ryan was up to that morning. Sure, some bridesmaid saw Laura getting friendly with Troy, but if I were the police, I'd put money on the killer being the jealous husband-to-be."

Jay looked satisfied with his answer. I tried to keep my mouth shut but found I couldn't let such a poorly thought-out theory lie. "You're suggesting he killed Troy in a jealous rage, right?"

"Yeah, exactly."

"With poison... a traditionally premeditated crime. Do the police even know how Troy was poisoned?" I asked, genuinely curious.

Jay shrugged. "I haven't heard anything. Heck, I guess you're right. I was thinking about the smashed up wedding cake, but I haven't heard anything about him being in a fight before he bit the dust." He frowned. "I dunno. Ryan's not too shabby in the brains department. He might have thought up something to shift the suspicion away from himself. And who's to say that what the bridesmaid saw was the first time?" He pointed a finger at me as if to say, aha!

I realised I had to concede that much. I'd been there for Ryan's reaction when he'd found out that his bride had been involved with his best man just hours before their wedding. It definitely hadn't been the first time something like it had happened... but had it been the first with Troy? I didn't think so. Someone had definitely mentioned the pair having a history that Ryan hadn't known about. Could that have changed things if he'd found out? "I'm sure the police will sort everything," I said - although I believed no such thing if Walter Miller was the one in charge. I could only hope that the Kingston Hill police department had taken on the murder case.

"I guess so. Until then, we'd better all sleep with one eye open."

I looked at Jay with some surprise. Everyone I'd spoken to up to this point had shared the assumption that Troy had done something which deservedly ended in his death. After all - he'd had a reputation. This was the first time anyone had suggested the killer might be looking to strike again.

"I don't think we're in any danger. It's nothing to do with us," I said, somehow feeling like a traitor to justice for saying it. But it was the truth, wasn't it? There was no need for any of us to get involved.

Jay shrugged. "Someone might know too much, you know?" He grinned. "Anyway, I'd better be getting on. Lena will need picking up from school in the blink of an eye and this time is all I get to accomplish anything."

I opened my mouth and then shut it again, not knowing if it was proper to ask what Jay did in order to make money to support his small family.

"I'm a copywriter," he supplied, clearly reading my expressions. "I wouldn't say it's thrilling work, but it pays the bills. Kerrie never thought I'd even be able to do that much with it, but when she left... what choice did I have?" He shrugged again, but it was less cheery.

"Was Kerrie your fiancée?" I asked and then had the good grace to blush as I realised I'd just repeated something I'd learned through neighbourhood gossip.

Jay looked more amused than annoyed. "People still talk about it, eh? Lena was five years old. I won't lie, things were pretty stressful during that time in terms of making ends meet. We were also trying to plan the cheapest wedding in history." He ran a rueful hand through his hair. "I guess it wasn't enough for Kerrie. One morning she went out to do the weekly shop and she didn't come back. Haven't heard from her since."

I felt my ears prick up. "You never heard from her again… ever? Did you report her missing?" I was all too conscious that I'd just concealed a skeleton in my lawnmower.

"Yeah, of course I did. I told the police and said where she'd gone. They looked into it, but as her car was missing, they decided she'd just run off, rather than been taken. They did their part but there were no leads. In the end, they just stopped looking. I was left with a choice of whether to wait around, hoping that she'd come back, or get on with my life. I decided to get on with it, for Lena's sake. She doesn't even really remember Kerrie now."

"It sounds to me like you're doing a great job of bringing her up," I trilled, trying not to think about the bones. How old had they looked? Pretty old, that was for sure. Would five years be enough time for full decomposition to occur inside the urn? I realised I was being stupid. There'd never been an actual body in there. The clear plastic bag looked as fresh as the day it had been bought. Nothing had rotted away in it.

What a horrible thought.

"You'll get to meet Lena when you come along to the party on Friday. I know we'll both be looking forward to it," Jay said with another easy smile.

I did my best to return it whilst wondering if his missing fiancée was in my lawnmower. "I can't wait!"

Jay flashed me another one of those happy looks that I didn't quite know how to interpret, but my thoughts were already elsewhere. I waited for him to walk back down the path that led out to the lane before I shut the workshop door and locked it again.

So, the old devil was a murderer! I thought, connecting the dots between the bones in Jim's planter and Jim himself. It just went to show, you never knew what kind of secrets people were keeping.

Except... I didn't think it was as simple as that.

Someone had searched my house... which meant someone else knew about the skeleton.

I marched over to the lawnmower's grass compartment and opened it. The bag of bones was waiting for me.

"Archaeological enthusiast with a penchant for collecting old bones?" I mused but I was lying to myself. I knew enough biology to realise that these bones were all part of the same skeleton. For one, there were still a few places where sinew remained, holding some of the joints together. Aside from that, they'd been picked clean. There was no way these bones had been anything other than bones when Jim had decided to store them in the bag. I peered closer at the bag itself and noticed that there were a few clumps of earth in the bottom. The bones, too, had some marks of being in the ground on them.

I opened the bag and delved inside, coming out with a broken rib... and then another one. There were serrated marks that hinted how the owner of the skeleton had met their end on the wrong end of what I assumed had been a pretty pointy knife.

I revised my opinion of Jim. I didn't think he was a murderer, but I did think he'd known who'd done it.

"Great," I muttered. The lawyer's words came back into my head: *"Anything inside it now belongs to you."* When she'd originally said it, there'd been this little hesitation that had come after as well, like she'd thought of adding something but had then thought better of it.

I frowned. Had this been what Georgina Farley had been referring to when she'd said that whatever was inside the property was mine to do what I wanted with? The skeleton hadn't actually been inside the house, but she might not have known the exact location.

"I should have known there's no such thing as a free lunch," I said to Diggory who lifted another sleepy ear before dropping it again. Jim Holmes had given me his house and land out of the blue when he'd died. I'd assumed he'd wanted to support my business idea (and also shown a healthy disdain for his surviving relatives) but now I was definitely starting to believe that there was more to it than that. Jim had known that one day someone would come looking for the skeleton. I thought he'd asked the lawyer to tip me off, so I would be as aware of the situation as possible - without incurring any legal problems. I wasn't sure just how much Georgina Farley actually knew, but I was pretty sure she wasn't clueless.

What it amounted to was Jim had swanned off the mortal coil and left me with a hot potato. Or in this case - a bag of bones, sans-skull.

I stowed the mystery of the missing skull as something to wonder about later.

For now, I was more interested in who, exactly, I was looking at.

I didn't have any memories of anyone going missing from the village, or the surrounding area. Jay's fiancée was the only current possible on my list. I bit my lip, knowing it didn't entirely fit my imagined profile. For one, the bones were clean and old. Even buried in the ground, it took a fair few years for full decomposition to occur, even if the soil was particularly favourable for that sort of thing. For just a moment, everything Fergus had said about there being strange things in our soil popped back into my head, but I shook the thought away. Evil soil or not, I wasn't certain that this was Kerrie. The bones were small enough to belong to a woman, but could I really afford to jump to conclusions yet? I measured the femur against my own and tried to guess the skeleton's height. *Even more reason to go to that party,* I thought, figuring I could pry more into Kerrie's appearance there.

"You should go straight to the police," I said out loud, looking at the bones and trying to behave in a logical manner.

A loud sigh escaped from my lips. I couldn't do it. Not only was I not exactly enamoured with the abilities of local law enforcement, I also had a strong feeling that dealing with this skeleton was part of the reason I'd been left the property in the first place. If Jim had wanted it to be turned over to the police, he'd have left something in his will that detailed where the skeleton could be found and who was responsible for it - only to be opened when he was dead. None of that had happened, so I could only assume that there was a good reason for him having the skeleton… and one that he wanted me to figure out without involving the police.

I leant back against the lawnmower, my thoughts a whirl of action. I needed to find out the identity of the skeleton. Then I'd be able to decide what to do next.

I looked from the bag of bones to the false terracotta urn and decided that I couldn't return them to their original hiding place. Perhaps no one implicated in the murder had witnessed me moving the urns around, but even if they didn't think I'd found anything, it could have given my burglar a fresh idea of where to hunt, if they had been watching. I would be a fool to stick the bones back where I'd found them.

An idea popped into my head. I'd had a wood-burning stove put in since coming to the house. It was one of the few luxuries I'd allowed myself - although I told myself it would be a necessity once winter rolled around again. When it had been put in, the workmen had needed to partially demolish the old, very large chimney and put in a metal flue instead. As a result, there was an alcove in the attic created by the void left behind by the original chimney. It was currently neatly covered in plasterboard. I'd been advised to either leave it like that, or have the entire thing plastered over, should I ever wish to convert the attic. I'd almost laughed out loud at the idea that I'd ever feel affluent enough to afford such an extravagance. The interior of the house as it stood was more than enough room for Diggory and myself, and I didn't see us adding to the family anytime soon.

However, if I shifted the board, the alcove would make a perfect hiding space - and one that would look too recent to have anything suspicious hidden behind it, courtesy of the previous resident.

Satisfied with my plan, I popped the plastic bag into a bag for life that had been left in the workshop. When the bag promptly disintegrated and dropped the bag of bones straight onto the floor, I cursed, and then settled on a thick, burlap sack. Those things were *really* bags for life…

Feeling like a criminal, I exited the workshop, walked down the gravel path, and then out onto the lane that led back to my house. My heart was hammering in my chest as I tried to stroll casually and discovered that I could hardly remember how to walk at all. I took a deep breath and then another, shutting my eyes for a moment and just wanting this terrifying trip to be over.

When I opened my eyes, I was met with a terrible sight.

There was a removal van parked in the middle of the lane. Three people had just jumped out of the cab.

"Oh, come on!" I muttered, peeved beyond all reason that now was the moment that a hoard of people would pick to materialise in the usually deserted lane. I hadn't even known that the house across the lane from mine was up for sale!

I took another deep breath to reassure myself that no one could see anything. I was just a woman with a burlap sack in one hand and a trowel in the other.

Darn. Could I have looked more suspicious if I'd tried? Why hadn't I picked something non-threatening, like a bucket, to carry? Trowels and burlap sacks were hardly the most innocent of companions. Perhaps Diggory would distract them with his 'I couldn't harm a fly' friendliness.

Double darn. I'd forgotten Diggory somewhere along the gravel path when he'd stopped to sniff an interesting tree stump.

"Diggory!" I shouted, turning back towards where I'd last seen my wayward dog.

I whipped my head back in the direction I was going, hoping to slip past the moving crew unnoticed.

I was just in time to see a police car pull into the space in front of the moving van. How had they known?! Had someone seen me finding the bones through the workshop window and turned me in? What kind of excuse did I have for walking around carrying them in a sack?! My breathing got a lot more shallow as panic started to take hold.

And then everything got a whole lot worse.

One of the people I'd seen getting out of the cab of the moving lorry walked around the back of the van and saw me. There was a dreadful moment when I made eye contact with him and realised it was none other than Spencer Byrne, the man I'd loved as a teenager. The man whose wedding I should never have gone to.

Because I was probably still in love with him.

6

THE BITTER TASTE OF MURDER

I slapped on a smile and watched an equally forced grin appear on Spencer's face. He wasn't thrilled to see me either. I wondered if Francesca had been the one to send out invitations? I hadn't been good friends with her, but with the last minute nature of the affair, perhaps they'd been pushed for people who were still living locally to invite.

As if I'd needed any more salt rubbing in the wound.

"What are you doing here?" I blurted, before realising that it was exceedingly obvious. Spencer and his new wife were moving into the house opposite mine.

"What are **you** doing here?" My words were echoed exactly by an all too familiar voice of someone else. It was then that I remembered the police car... and the family connection. How had I forgotten that Francesca Steele's uncle was none other than Detective Walter Miller.

I turned grudgingly to face the moustached law man. "I live here. There," I said, pointing with my trowel towards my house, in case he assumed that I lived out in the lane itself. I would not have put it past the man to draw such a stupid conclusion. I nearly added; 'remember when you tried to arrest me because Jim Holmes left me that house in his will?' but I hardly needed to tempt fate right now. Not when I was literally carrying a murder victim around in a bag.

"Huh," was all Walter had to say about that. I figured it meant he didn't approve of his niece's new neighbour. I was hardly over the moon myself.

"I should let you get on with the unpacking. I'm sure you have lots to do," I trilled, eager to get out of this dreadful and ridiculous situation. I thought I could almost feel the threads of the burlap coming unwound, ready to drop the see-through plastic bag of bones out onto the road at any moment.

"Yes," Walter Miller said and immediately walked past me to the back of the van, wrenching the doors open and noisily rifling around back there.

Spencer looked at me for a long and awkward few seconds. He opened his mouth to say something but at that very moment his new wife rounded the corner.

"Spencer... Ooo look at that dog! He's got a bone! How sweet," she said, changing tack halfway through whatever she'd been about to say.

I turned away from the new Mrs Byrne and saw Diggory trotting down the lane towards us, having finally heeded my call.

There was a big yellow bone in his mouth.

It looked like the femur I'd examined earlier.

Darn! I must have forgotten to put it back in the sack!

"Is it still safe to give dogs bones these days?" Francesca continued, smiling from Spencer to me, apparently oblivious about the tense situation she'd just walked in on. I felt a bead of sweat slide down the back of my neck. I'd been reluctant to hand over the bones in part due to my perception of

Walter Miller's incompetence as a detective, but surely even he would recognise a human bone?

"Big ones are fine. That one came from a cow," I covered, knowing it was the only thing big enough to pass muster.

"Well, there you go!" Francesca said, rubbing her large belly.

I wondered when it was due. By the looks of it, it had to be any day now.

"What are you doing around here, Diana? I didn't get to say hi to you at the wedding…"

"I, uh, had to rush off I'm afraid. My house was broken-in to," I said, before wishing I'd thought up something better. How would I have known it had been burgled prior to returning home?

Fortunately, everyone present had stopped listening after I'd uttered the words 'broken-in'.

"Crime? There's crime in this neighbourhood?" Walter Miller pulled his head back out of the truck so fast I thought he might crick his back.

"Well… nothing was actually taken. It was just a broken window really," I said, downplaying it as much as I could. Another bead of sweat broke loose and slid down my back. Diggory unhelpfully plonked himself down next to me, the bone still wedged in his mouth, in full-view of Detective Walter Miller.

The detective was preoccupied with the possibility that his niece could have just moved into a crime-stricken area. At this moment in time, I didn't want to draw his attention away from that idea.

"I suppose that could just be called petty vandalism rather than burglary, but there is the murder to consider." I turned to Francesca, feeling mean for doing it, but hey - I was desperate! "I did the flowers for the wedding of the couple who live just behind me. Their best man was murdered at the wedding! All of the neighbours were questioned," I said, borrowing from Jay's own exaggeration.

"It was Troy Wayland who got himself topped. That's been in the pipeline since... well... ever since he started causing trouble!" the detective protested, spitting feathers over the sensationalism.

I shrugged like it was still up in the air. Which, to my knowledge, it actually was. "I'm sure it's nothing to worry about. Happy new home!" I said and then hurried on down the lane.

Somehow I doubted I'd be invited to the housewarming party.

Once inside my house, I breathed the biggest sigh of relief ever, before realising I'd forgotten Diggory again. I threw the front door open and yanked him inside, confiscating the bone. "Thanks a lot, trouble," I told my dog who shot me an oblivious doggy grin and slowly wagged his tail.

I took a few more deep breaths whilst I waited for my heart rate to return to a level normal in humans. Then I went upstairs and put up the loft ladder. Five minutes later, the plastic bag of bones, including the now-slightly-chewed femur, was safely stowed behind the boards left behind by the wood-burner crew. I knew it wouldn't be a great idea to leave the bones and bag next to a flue that would probably get hot when I actually used the burner, but winter still felt a long way off, and I wasn't intending to hang onto the bones indefinitely, was I?

I sat down against the boarded-up alcove and thought about everything I knew and everything else that I needed to find out.

My first observation was that I'd been left a cursed inheritance, and I believed the lawyer involved had known something about it. I would definitely need to make contact with her in case any further instructions had been left. I wasn't sure if Jim Holmes had told Georgina Farley the whole truth (would she have been obligated to report it to the police, or was there some code of silence for lawyers?) but he'd sure as heck hinted that something wasn't right. I considered the only other heir to Jim's inheritance and thought I could see why I'd been chosen to deal with the problem. Going by the dim view I'd formed of his grand-daughter, Nina Holmes, she'd have sold the property - probably without even seeing it first. The skeleton problem would have been passed onto someone else, who (if they found it) would almost certainly report it to the police without asking questions first. I thought that Jim had left subtle hints behind for a reason. He'd wanted someone to know the truth.

I shut my eyes and considered the questions running around in my head.

How had the skeleton ended up in the planter?

Who had been the killer?

How long had the skeleton been in the fake terracotta urn?

I rubbed a hand across my aching temples. The only thing I knew for sure was that someone else knew about the skele-ton. Or at least - I assumed that was what they'd been searching for.

Unless there was something else hidden in the house.

I shook my head, hoping that wasn't the case. I'd had more than enough bad surprises for one day. Even as I thought about the bag of bones behind the boards, I wondered if it was somehow connected to the far more recent murder of Troy Wayland. I couldn't immediately see how the two could possibly be connected, but it was certainly something to think on. After all - the burglary had occurred the day before he was murdered. Someone had dug up my land, too, I remembered. I shook my head, remem-bering that Fergus hadn't exactly denied being responsible for that incident. Even so... something was definitely in the air around here.

Or in the soil, I silently thought, remembering Fergus' ludicrous claims. I rolled my eyes upwards to the heavens. Was I really considering giving that man the time of day? I'd done some research on him when I hadn't been able to sleep after the wedding. I'd been surprised to discover that Fergus had allegedly once worked as a member of a security service. Once I'd got over my surprise, I'd regarded it with suspicion. The terminology was vague and I reckoned that it could mean anything from working as supermarket security to working as some kind of government agent. I'd snorted at the thought of Fergus being a secret agent and had dismissed the idea.

The website his information was listed on was a site called 'The Truth Beneath'. A skim read had merely confirmed what I'd already assumed. Fergus was a conspiracy theorist. He was a member of a group of other conspiracy theorists, who believed some very strange things about the planet we inhabit... and as far as I could tell, without a single shred of scientific evidence to back up any of these claims.

Until someone showed me a chemical analysis that said I was wrong about the soil here, I would not be giving over any time at all to Fergus Robinson's madcap theories.

The sound of a lorry reversing cut through the still air in the attic. I walked over to one of the dormer windows and watched as the removal van backed up the driveway opposite my house, presumably to reduce the distance they needed to haul everything.

It was only then that I realised how much trouble I was in. I'd literally just walked past the local chief of police carrying bones I strongly suspected belonged to a murder victim. And I'd done absolutely nothing about it. Even if I went down there right now and handed over the bag, I'd behaved strangely enough to warrant some serious questions and possibly even punishment. I could only reassure myself that I was certain the bones were old. It wasn't really the same as finding a corpse stuffed into a planter and knowing that there were probably people worrying about the person's wellbeing right this instant. Anyway, I didn't like not knowing what I was dealing with... and it wasn't as if I'd been the one to kill the mystery victim.

"Now what?" I said as I watched a car pull into my driveway. The engine stopped and the driver's door opened. I watched as a woman with dyed red hair stepped out. The passenger door opened a second later and a man dressed in a suit joined her on the gravel. I wasted a further moment wondering just what Nina Holmes was doing on my property when she was essentially banned from the local area, before I realised I needed to get out of the attic. With a skeleton hidden in my chimney, I couldn't be too careful.

I made it down the stairs just as the doorbell rang.

"What can I do for you?" I said when I answered the door and came face to face with the woman I'd believed had destroyed my cut flower business dreams forever.

"Quite a lot, actually," Nina said, a smug smile already firmly instated on her face. "The new place is looking good. My grandfather really did you a favour, didn't he?"

I bit my tongue to keep from saying that the presentable state of the property was due to my own hard graft and some careful spending of the money Jim had left. I doubted Nina was in the listening mood.

"I thought you were barred from Merryfield and the surrounding area?" I deliberately looked past the couple standing on my doorstep to the police car, prominently parked in the lane outside. Walter Miller may not be good for much, but for once, his presence could be a good thing.

"This hamlet isn't Merryfield, is it? And the boundaries were never really defined," Nina replied, even smugger than before. I wondered if it had taken her all of these months to figure that much out.

"What do you want?" I asked, seeing as my more polite initial question had been ignored.

"This is my lawyer, Jed Banks. We're here to make an account of the property and everything inside it, so that we can make sure everything is rightfully handed over to me," Nina explained.

"You're contesting the will? Now?" I asked, wanting to clarify.

Nina practically preened. "Yes, I am. It was never fair that he left all of that to you. You clearly brainwashed him or coerced him during the time you spent on your filthy allotments together. All of this should be mine. Jed thinks it should be a piece of cake to get the will thrown out." Her eyes glittered as she tried to look past me into the house at the cosy interior I'd worked so hard to make into a home.

I looked from Nina to the man dressed in the cheap suit and back again. "Good luck with that," I said and shut the door in their faces.

I heard Nina's exclamation of disgust on the other side of the door. Next, she asked her 'lawyer' if I was allowed to bar her from snooping around the property. He soothingly assured her they'd be able to obtain a court order in no time. I arched my eyebrows, figuring that 'in no time' was this lawyer's catch phrase. I didn't like to judge people solely on their appearances, but I didn't think that I was facing any real threat from this hack lawyer that Nina had dredged up from somewhere or other. All the same, it was probably worth phoning Georgina Farley to warn her that Nina Holmes had finally decided to contest the will. At the very least, it would give Georgina something to laugh about... and I needed to have a word with her anyway, didn't I?

The lawyer answered after a couple of rings. I explained the Nina Holmes situation and, just as I'd predicted, Georgina found the whole thing terribly amusing. She asked for the name of the 'lawyer' and when I told her, she made further sounds of amusement. Jed Banks had apparently tried to apply for a job at the law firm she'd first cut her teeth with. He was a little younger than she was, but when his apprenticeship was up, he'd been let go for being lazy and not bothering to check his facts. Since then, she didn't think he'd managed to join up with any reputable law firm. That was apparently the problem with studying to be a lawyer. Those who got a good degree and then managed to land a good job were assured of excellent money and healthy career prospects, but boy, was it competitive. Degrees in law were apparently two a penny. This Jed Banks character was apparently the dark side of what happened when you failed to make the grade.

"He'll run for the hills as soon as he discovers that I was the one who wrote the will his client is trying to contest," she assured me.

"I didn't think I had anything to worry about. I just thought I should warn you that they might be banging down your office door very soon."

"Thanks for the heads-up. I'm sure it will make an amusing divergence from the day I've got planned." For a moment, the lawyer sounded tired. I reflected that no matter the career you picked, if you wanted to be a success in your field, you needed to put the work in.

"There was something else I wanted to ask you," I began, ready to broach the subject of the skeleton in the planter, without explicitly mentioning that there had been a skeleton in the planter. "Was there a note or anything left with you?

Something that might be handed to the new owner of the property a year or so after they've settled in? A letter, maybe?"

"I'm afraid there's nothing like that," the lawyer answered, but I thought I detected a note of sympathy in her voice. She knew something.

I tried again. "Did Jim mention any, uh... surprises that might have been left on the property?"

"I'm afraid I have no idea," Georgina Farley answered, sounding a lot more prim and proper. "Anything in or on the property belongs to you, and it's up to you to decide what you do with it," she told me, slightly rewording what she'd said when we'd first seen the house together but retaining the sentiment. She hadn't known whether the skeleton was inside or outside of the house itself, and perhaps she didn't even know that 'it' was a skeleton, but she'd definitely been made aware that there was something fishy about my inheritance.

"Great. Thanks for the help," I said, not brilliantly impressed.

"I'll handle Nina Holmes and Jed Banks. I doubt you'll be hearing from either of them again." The lawyer was hoping to extend an olive branch at the close of our conversation. I courteously thanked her for her assistance, in a more civil way, and then hung up.

So, Jim had left me to deal with his problem without bothering to leave so much as a hint of where to begin. I very nearly threw my hands up and marched over to turn myself in and the bones over to the police, but the thought of admitting that I'd acted wrongly to Walter Miller stopped me.

I needed to think rationally about all of this. I put all thoughts of Nina Holmes and her sham lawyer and Spencer and his new wife out of my head and thought. I was a scientist. I needed to think like one.

The planters. When I'd discovered the bag of bones, I hadn't been too interested in what else, if anything, they might have contained.

With Diggory bouncing happily by my side I marched towards the front door, thought better of it, and then left via the backdoor, choosing to go the long way through my fields and jump a hedge over the prospect of bumping into the newlyweds again.

Once back in the workshop, I inspected the empty urn with its false bottom. If you didn't include cobwebs, there was absolutely nothing inside.

With a sigh, I plonked the planter back down. Then I looked at the other one. The tea tree was yanked out and tossed into another empty planter. Then the urn was flipped over. The bottom of this urn was still intact, but there was something there. A plastic folder had been taped in place. With a thumping heart, I pulled out the single piece of paper enclosed in the folder.

It was a receipt for the pair of planters, dated four years ago. I'd been hoping for a note from Jim, but as I thought about it, this was a clue. It let me know a time frame for the skeleton being added to the urn. Sometime during the three and a bit years prior to his death, Jim had dug up a skeleton from somewhere, inexplicably without a skull, and had neatly packaged the bones and concealed them in his fake terracotta urn.

Beyond that, I was clueless.

I tried to keep clear of the front of my house in the days that followed. It was only when I'd seen him in the church and again just outside my house that I'd realised I'd never resolved my feelings for Spencer Byrne. Deep down, I knew it was childish. I didn't even know the man that well - not then, and not now. When I'd been a teenager, I'd built a whole world around what he was and could be to me, and it was an illusion I was still under today. I knew it would shatter in an instant. I just hoped that the instant would happen soon.

Even though my life felt like it was in turmoil at the moment, business still continued as normal. It had to, or I'd be bankrupt and back at the laboratory with my tail between my legs in no time at all. Today I was making plans for the future by walking the boundary of my property and taking stock of exactly what needed to be done in order to tame the rest of the land Jim had left me. I also thought I should double-check exactly where the boundaries were - considering that there had been more than one trespassing incident of late - when you included the mysterious burglary and the digging.

Clouds were just starting to creep across the sky when I started my trek. Jim had left me one and a bit hectares of land, split into three different fields. The smallest field, which was also the one nearest to the house, I'd already attacked with heavy-duty gardening gear and transformed into my flower growing field and polytunnel site. The second was the largest field and was flanked by my neighbours Alice and Tom, and on the other side, the local paper editor, Samara - who I had yet to meet beyond occasional waves when our cars passed in the lane.

I walked along the hedgerow, observing the digging that Alice had pointed out and then walking on. Nothing more had been done at that particular site. I heard the sound of someone cursing. A second later, fat droplets of rain started to fall. Diggory gleefully barked and ran around the meadow of unruly dock leaves and brambles, mingled with some plucky wild grasses. I poked my head over the lowest point of the hedge to see if someone was in trouble.

"Oh! Hello there!" my neighbour said, looking shamefaced to discover he'd been overheard. "Sorry, the rain caught me by surprise. My wife Alice has told me all about you. You're Diana, right?" The man who'd done the cursing was dressed in dark blue swim shorts and had a torso with enough oil on it to fry a family-sized serving of chips. To be fair to him, he probably needed all the basting he could get when it came to getting a tan in our British summer.

"You're Tom, aren't you?" I said to the fair-haired man. I'd already spoken to Alice several times but her husband had been more elusive until now. I assumed it was because of his career.

"That's me! I was, uh… just taking a break from writing the next novel," he said, looking even more shamefaced. "Alice works in the days. It's when I get most of my writing done," he confided, flashing me a bright grin. He had the cheekbones of a cover model and steel-coloured eyes that probably stopped women in their tracks.

I privately thought that he could do with taking a break from sunbathing to write his novel, but I was willing to allow that I was a bit of a workaholic. I always had been.

"What sort of books do you write?" I asked, figuring it was about time I got to know my neighbours better than the gossip shared by others about them.

"Crime stuff. Thrillers, mostly. It's the kind of throwaway novel that people read on a flight, you know? Not exactly highbrow, but people seem to like them. Hopefully, when I've got a couple more books out…" He cleared his throat, regretting saying so much. "Alice is really supportive," he tacked on, knowing that I'd have worked out who the breadwinner in the family currently was. Looking at Tom, I thought I could understand why Alice was willing to go along with it.

"I'd like to read one of them," I told him sincerely. I didn't usually much go in for reading fiction, but I'd decided I did want to fit into my neighbourhood - no matter what certain unnamed people may think about it. I wanted to be accepted into the local community and beyond that, I wanted people to like me. Being liked would definitely give me the edge in my business of choice, or any business for that matter. People buy from people they like, and I was painfully aware that I sometimes came across as aloof and fact-focused rather than warm and fuzzy. It was something I was trying to work on.

"I've got loads of paperback copies lying around the house. I'll have to bring one over. Or get Alice to bring one over," Tom amended. I silently wondered if he didn't actually get out that much. That would make sense. I'd realised that it had been Alice and Alice alone who'd cared for the lawn when Jim Holmes had left the property and moved to Merryfield.

"Alice told you about our renters, didn't she?" Tom said, brightening up at the prospect of not talking about his writing.

"She did. I said it was absolutely fine. You're a long way away from my house anyway. I think your renter would be hard pressed to make any nuisance of themselves." I smiled at the man. He looked away, taking a long drink from the glass of coke that was being rained on. I glanced at the caramel coloured liquid and noted that it looked a lot lighter than normal coke - and I doubted the rain was to blame. There was definitely more to Tom than met the eye.

"We've got our first Airbnb client coming this weekend. We used to have longer term lets, but the market has changed like you wouldn't believe. It's going to really help pay the bills," he said and then blushed anew. Tom was letting all kinds of things slip today, and I was willing to hazard a guess that it was to do with whatever it was that he'd mixed into his coke.

"I hope it goes well. Perhaps I could do something similar one day…" I said thinking of the workshop that seldom saw use. If I converted it, would it be worth it?

Tom nodded enthusiastically. "Oh, you definitely should! I could tell you everything there is to know." He beamed at me, forgetting whatever hesitancy there'd been earlier. "Airbnb have got some great insurance policies, too, just in case something goes wrong and your place gets trashed." He pulled a face. "I'm sure that won't happen to us. All of our applicants so far have been middle-aged couples and singles looking to get away into the Sussex countryside. We're hardly a party destination out here in the sticks, are we?"

I smiled my agreement.

"It was different before this short term thing was accessible to everyone. We rented for longer and for cheaper. That didn't always end so well. One tenant had to be evicted by court order because she refused to leave when her tenancy was up. Believe me - there's nothing more awkward than suing someone who lives above your garage. In the end, we let her skip her final payment if it got her out of our hair." He shook his head. "In the end, she just disappeared one night with everything she could grab that wasn't nailed down and left us out of pocket." He shook his head. "We were suckers back then."

"That's terrible! Weren't the police able to do anything?"

Tom let out a barking laugh before looking embarrassed and taking another swig from his alcohol and coke. "You know what Old Bill is like around here. If there was a mafia syndicate murdering people in public and a little old lady who forgot to pay a parking fine, I bet they'd focus on the little old lady."

"Low hanging fruit," I muttered, feeling much the same

about the local police force. I considered adding a potential candidate for the body. The tenant might have disappeared in a more permanent fashion than her landlords realised.

"Hey, did you know that Samara and Jay are getting together in secret?" Tom said, brightening up once more. "I write in an office we made up in the attic. I've been seeing Samara sneak out across her garden and your field..." he coughed, realising he'd just dropped our neighbour in it for trespassing. "I'm sure she doesn't mean anything by it. For the past week, she's been knocking on Jay's back door and being let in. I guess they're shacking up together."

"Why would they want to keep it a secret?" I wondered out loud.

"Well, they've both got kids, haven't they?" Tom said. "Although Samara's girl grew up and left after all of her troubles... But still... it's a big decision to make an affair into something more public. I hope it works out between them. Otherwise, we'll have more neighbourly feuds on our hands."

"Who's feuding with who?" I asked, wondering if I really had landed in a terrible neighbourhood.

Tom pulled a face. "I suppose no one is now..." he looked uncomfortable. "Nothing much has happened since Jim upped sticks and left a couple years back. Alice and I always got on okay with Jim, apart from one thing where he'd planted some hydrangeas way over our boundary where the hedge used to come to an end right down the bottom of the field." He pointed to show the place. "But we resolved it civilly. However, I can't say the same for the rest of our neighbours. Samara and Jim had a really big bust up a few years ago over a tree. It was on the border between her garden and Jim's field. Samara said the roots were interfering with her property and it needed to be cut down. He declined permission. A week later, the tree was mysteriously vandalised with a chain saw." He shot me a knowing look.

"Samara claimed to know nothing about it. Jim never believed her." Tom shrugged. "She wasn't the only one that Jim rubbed up the wrong way. Laura and Ryan complained about Jim letting his fields run wild and ruining their property's value. To get his own back, Jim decided to have a bonfire at the same time the couple were having a garden party one summer. The wind just happened to be blowing their way when Jim decided to throw some old plastic lawn furniture on the fire. They called the police and threatened to report him for trying to poison them."

I made a thoughtful expression in response. It was true that burning particular plastics and other synthetic materials could sometimes form hydrogen cyanide gas as a by-product of their combustion. However, cyanide usually needed high temperatures and low-oxygen environments to form, and even if some had been released, it was unlikely to have had any ill effects out in the open air. Something in my brain had just lit up, but I wasn't sure what it was trying to tell me.

"Then he argued with Mrs Bellefleur, who's our furthest neighbour." He pointed towards the big house in the distance, nearest to the main road that led to Merryfield. "That was because she beat him in some vegetable competition or other." That sounded like Jim. "Before all of that, he fell out with Jay. That was pretty awful."

"What did they fall out over?" I hardly dared to ask.

Tom opened his mouth to answer, but at that moment the back door opened and Alice walked out into the garden. I pretended not to notice when Tom discreetly tipped the remainder of his glass of coke and fun onto the grass.

"Hello everyone! Why are we all hanging out in the rain?" she asked, approaching with an inquisitive smile on her face. As soon as she got close to Tom she frowned, probably smelling the haze of alcohol that still hung around, despite Tom's best attempts.

"It only just started raining, darling. I was just taking a break from writing," he explained.

Alice's subtly arched eyebrow was all the confirmation I needed that I was correct about my earlier hypothesis on Tom's taking of breaks. "What were you chatting about?"

"Tom was telling me about all the trouble Jim caused when he lived here. I'm so sorry," I said, feeling as though I needed to apologise for the mean-heartedness of my property's predecessor.

"I don't like to speak ill of the dead, but I'm sure there are many around here who think the way Jim Holmes met his end was a case of just desserts." Alice looked down at Diggory when she said it. My doggy companion just wagged his tail and looked thrilled with himself. "I know we were all hoping for a quieter, friendlier neighbourhood when he left, but it hasn't really turned out that way, has it?" She shot me a weak smile.

"I suppose not," I said, gloomily thinking of the newest neighbours to move to the hamlet, just across the road from me.

"Did you hear the news? The man who died, Troy, he was poisoned by a cigarette, of all things," Alice revealed, looking suitably horrified. "Apparently, it contained crystals of…"

"…cyanide," I completed, remembering the last lingering smell of bitter almonds. I must have had my head in the clouds that day to not realise the smell hadn't come from the cake but from the cigarette itself. It was Tom's talk of Jim's plastic bonfire that had caused something to jolt in my brain, and now I knew why.

"Yes! How did you know?" Alice asked, looking curious and then slightly suspicious.

"Walter Miller's niece has just moved in opposite me," I said and was relieved when those listening seemed to accept my statement as an explanation for my knowledge. It was simpler than explaining the truth of my knowledge and probably making myself look more like a likely suspect in the process. "I hope they find out who killed him."

Alice and Tom both nodded. "I hope nothing else bad happens," Tom said, sounding gloomy.

"It's not as bad as all that! The way I heard it, this murder is nothing to do with anyone around here. It's all the stuff Troy must have stirred up when he went off to the city," Alice interjected.

Tom didn't look reassured. "But what about the break-ins?"

"Break-ins?" I queried, picking up on his use of a plural.

"I didn't tell you?" Tom looked mortified and then glanced down at his empty glass. The culprit, I assumed. "We were broken into just the other day. I reported it to the police and the guy who came out said that it was just the same as what apparently happened to you a few days ago. Nothing was actually taken, but the backdoor lock had been forced." He blushed. "I was actually at home at the time. Alice was at work and I, ah… must have drifted off for a nap. At least there was no harm really done, but it's disturbing, isn't it?"

"Did you find any scratch marks? Any floorboards or carpets levered up?" I asked, wondering if it could be the work of the same person.

"Now that you mention it, yes," Alice said with a frown. "It was only today that I noticed. Someone moved our wardrobe out from the wall - there were marks on the carpet. I also noticed one of our flagstones had been prised up in the kitchen. It was loose anyway. We've been meaning to get it fixed, but there were scrape marks when I looked this morning. I hadn't put two and two together until now. Should we add it to our crime report?"

"Perhaps," I said, now certain that whoever had broken-in

to my house had also been the one to invade Tom and Alice's home. "I think we should ask around. It might be more than just us who's been broken-in to. Or if not yet… they might be next on the culprit's list."

"But why would they break-in but not take anything? Do you think its vandals?" Tom said, looking baffled.

"Vandals who like to rearrange the furniture?" Alice shot Tom a bemused look.

"I think they're looking for something," I said, keeping my voice level and my expression a blank slate. I didn't want anyone to know that I had already found the item I strongly suspected this burglar had been hunting for. Especially now I was fast getting the idea that the searcher didn't even know who had the skeleton.

"But what?" Tom said, looking equal parts curious and confused.

"It could be something to do with the murder," Alice said, making a leap of logic that I, too, was considering.

"It could be," I echoed. "But I was broken-in to the day before Troy died."

After that, it seemed like there was nothing much more to be said. None of us really knew what was going on in our neighbourhood, or even if these two crimes were connected. All we could do was remark upon the dismal state of affairs and get on with our small-town lives. I had a boundary to walk and plans to make, and Alice had a husband to sober up.

I definitely knew whose job I preferred.

Later that evening, I still found myself wondering what Jim Holmes and Jay had fought about. Lena's tenth birthday and party was tomorrow, but I wasn't sure it was really the occasion to try to find out.

I sighed and looked down at the plans I'd sketched out for the bouquet. I was going for something that would appeal to the girly girl that Jay had hinted she was - pinks and candy colours galore, courtesy of my hardy gerbera crop, but with a couple of 'grown up' sprigs of eucalyptus and a few dainty, but perfectly formed, deep pink roses. I had a feeling it was going to look stunning and smell amazing. I couldn't wait to hand it over to the young girl.

I thought back to my conversation with Jay when he'd ordered the bouquet and decided I still wasn't sure if I'd imagined his interest. He and Samara may have something going on at the moment, but if his eyes were wandering else-where, it may not have long left to run. I decided there and then that I wasn't going to stay long at the party. I didn't want to step on anybody's toes, and I very definitely didn't want to be the cause of a brand new neighbourly feud. I would hand over the bouquet, stay long enough to not be considered rude, and then excuse myself.

Unfortunately, these practical thoughts weren't enough to distract me from speculating about the skeleton I was keeping in my attic and all that I'd learned today. Jim had always been cantankerous when I'd known him, but if the reports were true, then he'd mellowed in his final year or so. "Or perhaps he got beyond the influence of the evil compost," I muttered, before snorting in derision.

Even if the Jim I'd known was nicer than the man my new neighbours had been accustomed to, I couldn't imagine him killing the absconding renter that Tom had mentioned. I wasn't even sure that the skeleton in my attic was the missing renter. Tom had said 'she', and I really did think these bones belonged to a female. But I had no clue beyond it being a vague possibility.

The spate of burglaries was also food for thought. It was both alarming and comforting in equal parts. Someone was desperately searching for the skeleton - of that much I was close to completely certain. However, they had no idea which of their neighbours had it. I spared a thought to wonder what had made them suspect their neighbours, and why they'd decided to search now - years after I believed the skeleton had been concealed in the urn, but I could find no satisfactory answer yet.

I sighed again as I climbed the ladder into the loft and looked at the stack of floriculture journals Jim had left me in his will. I'd found a desk and a chair already in situ when I'd moved in and could only assume that Jim had used the loft for the same office purpose as I did. The journals had remained piled up where I'd found them. I'd leafed through a couple and had made a mental note to come back to them if I needed flower ideas, but what modern shoppers wanted in a bouquet, and what had been in vogue at the time Jim had been growing flowers, were - for the most part - two very different things. Brides made the demands, and the flower growers struggled to keep up. It was just the way it was - unless you were a trendsetter who held influence within your field. I was definitely nowhere near that stage yet.

For a moment I looked from my laptop with its cashflow forecast and lengthy to-do list of actions I needed to take to drum up business, back to the pile of dusty, dog-eared journals. I knew what I should be spending my time on.

But that didn't stop me from reaching for the journals.

Jim had left me money, a house, and everything inside it, but he'd left his floriculture journals to me as a separate bequest. My old allotments friend Deirdre had received the vegetable journals, but I'd been left those detailing the flowers Jim had grown - flowers I'd never even guessed he'd cared about. Could the specification that the flower journals went to me be the clue I'd been hoping had been left behind?

Jim had planned his will carefully, so it stood to reason that he'd planned for the skeleton, too.

I opened the first journal and started to read. Did the truth about the headless skeleton reside somewhere between the yellowing pages? I had a feeling I was about to find out.

7

BARKIMEDES

I woke up with my head in a dusty book. Blinking, I realised I must have fallen asleep at my desk last night whilst poring over the floriculture journals. So far, I'd learned a heck of a lot about moon cycle seed sowing and the best local natural fertiliser sources but nothing at all about any skeletons. However, I was only two books in and there were another ten to get through. I'd also never seen such tiny writing. Jim had definitely got his money's worth from the little journals.

When I'd started reading, I'd hoped there would be some sort of chronology to the books, or even some kind of order at all, but there was nothing of the sort. Jim had written recipes for plant food and pest deterrent, notes about the land, and successes and failures in his flower growing in a seemingly random fashion. The only hint were the multitude of sticky tabs that stuck out of the books with specific plants and topics named. It was as though every time he'd had a thought or found something out, he'd noted it down... without bothering with a date or anything like that. I had no idea how long these journals spanned, or even if I was reading the most recent one. The only way forward would be to read through them all.

But not right now, I realised, seeing the time flash up on my iPad. I'd slept late. It was nearly beyond peak flower-gathering time. I had a bouquet to pick and plans to make for tomorrow's market. The detective work would have to wait.

The party was in full swing when I arrived carrying my bouquet. The birthday girl was sitting at the head of the table and, as promised, there was jelly and ice-cream being dished out by the boatload. I hovered in the doorway for a moment, having walked in through the open front door past the signs that said 'party!'. Jay looked up from the giant tray of ice-cream and jelly he was holding and smiled warmly at me.

"Lena… there's a special delivery here for you," he said, speaking to the birthday girl. She turned and looked at me with curious dark eyes.

"Is it your birthday today?" I asked, bending down and smiling at her.

She nodded, shyness taking her tongue.

"How old are you?" As if I were oblivious to the double digits displayed on shiny banners all around the room.

"I'm ten!" she told me proudly.

"That's an important age," I said, my voice solemn. "It needs an important gift." I whisked the bouquet out from behind my back and presented it to her.

The little girl's eyes grew wide. "Flowers? Just for me?"

I nodded. "Just for you. From…" I looked up in time to see Jay wink and shake his head. Apparently ten was old enough to consider it not cool to get a nice present from your dad in front of your friends.

"…From someone who thinks you're very special," I told

her. I thought I saw the glimmer of understanding in her eyes when I said it - ten year olds could be very smart - but she just grinned and thanked me.

"They're so pretty," she said in awe and then showed her friends, who crowded around making jealous sounds. Jay had been right about his choice of gift.

"Come on now... I'm sure those flowers need water to keep them looking pretty. We'll take them to the kitchen and Diana can tell me exactly what to do," Jay said, stepping in before the bouquet got too mangled by the many inquisitive hands.

I followed the happy father into the kitchen and politely accepted the bowl of jelly and ice-cream he offered me on the way. To my surprise, the kitchen wasn't empty.

"Hi," the woman standing next to the counter dishing up yet more jelly and ice-cream said. She gave me a look up and down, and I could instantly tell that I was being measured up. A flash of uncertainty crossed her expression, telling me that my hypothesis about the state of Jay's current relationship was correct.

"You're Samara, aren't you? We've been driving past each other for months," I said with what I hoped was a friendly and non-threatening smile.

"You're Diana. It's good to meet you at last. I've heard a lot about you," the other woman said, brushing her dark curling hair back off her face. She was in her thirties, I estimated, and had an exotic look about her. Her skin was already showing a tan in the early summer weather and her dark eyes and hair made her look as though she had Spanish origins. I bet I looked like a ghost next to her.

"I'm just gonna grab a vase and put these in water," I said when the silence stretched out a little too long. "Have you got a vase?" I asked, the thought suddenly striking me. Jay was a single father, and although he had every right to like having flowers around the house and own vases, I wouldn't be completely surprised if there weren't any.

"Oh, sure," he said, rustling up a perfectly serviceable china vase. He maintained eye contact with me as he handed it over.

I felt a blush rise to my cheeks and looked down at the vase, determined not to give him any reaction, beyond what my ridiculous cheeks were doing. Whatever was going on between Jay and Samara I did not want to get in-between it.

Not when I suspected I may be living in a neighbourhood that harboured at least one murderer.

"There we go!" I said, two minutes later. The flowers looked great. I was sure they were going to last a good long time, too, with proper care. I politely, but succinctly, informed Jay exactly what he needed to do to keep them fresh, doing my best to ignore the little smiles he kept trying to shoot me whenever Samara's attention was focused elsewhere.

"I'm afraid I've got to be getting home. Diggory destroys things when he's left on his own for too long," I invented. Diggory's days of destruction were actually long behind him. He'd been making up for lost time spent lazing ever since I'd had him as a pet. "Plus, I don't like leaving the house for too long at the moment... ever since someone broke in."

Samara lifted her head from doing some washing up and looked at me. "You were broken-in to?"

"Yes." I'd assumed that the hamlet gossip chain would have supplied that information to everyone by now, but apparently I was wrong about how chatty the locals were. Perhaps I was the only one they talked to because I was the new girl. I didn't come with years worth of feuds and baggage.

"My house was broken-in to last night when I was at a newspaper awards ceremony. It's the strangest thing..."

"...nothing was taken," I finished for her. "It was exactly the same for both me and Tom and Alice when they were burgled."

Samara's eyes widened. "It happened to them, too?"

We both turned to look at Jay.

He shrugged and lifted his hands up. "If I'm being honest with you, the door to this place is left wide open most of the time. I doubt I'd notice whether or not someone had broken-in."

"Have you got any big cupboards or wardrobes?" I asked.

Jay looked mystified but he took us up to a bedroom and pointed to the large antique-looking wardrobe that was there. I bent down and looked at the carpet for a while before finding what I was looking for. "Scrape marks. Someone tried to drag this out on their own to see what was behind it."

"Should there be something behind it?" Jay asked, looking more baffled by the second.

"Someone thought there might be," I said with grim certainty before remembering I probably shouldn't sound so dour. All of this was a curious mystery rather than something murderous, as far as my listeners were concerned. They didn't know that I'd discovered a headless skeleton.

"I suppose I should report it to the police..." Jay was saying when I stopped considering the implications of these further break-ins.

"Make sure you get Daniel Herald rather than Walter Miller," I advised. Then, whilst they were still focused on the marks on the carpet and the excitement of a real-life burglar, I made my excuses and slipped out of the party.

If I never saw jelly and ice-cream again it would be too soon.

There was a dog waiting at my house when I arrived back. He was sitting patiently on my doorstep with a lost look about him. When I walked up the path, he turned towards me and gave his tail a hopeful wag. I bent down and spoke softly to the brown and white canine. He looked like a Heinz 57 type... which is to say - a little bit of everything. He had smooth white short hair with big brown spots and his tail curled up in a humorous looking corkscrew. After a moment of consideration, the mystery dog walked over and allowed me to pat him.

"Let's find out where you're from, shall we?" I said, reaching for the collar the dog was wearing. At least someone knew the importance of keeping personal information attached to their pets, just in case they should ever get lost.

I looked down at the metal tag and then dialled the number listed. It rang, but there was no answer on the other end.

"Come on, let's get you inside. I bet you're thirsty," I said to the uncertain dog. The tail wagged again as I opened the door.

Diggory was sitting right behind it. Silent and staring.

I jumped and then glared at my pet. "What do you think you're doing, giving me a fright like that?"

He looked from me to the dog and back again. Then, to my surprise, he gave a little growl.

I stuck my hands on my hips and gave him a stern look. "Now look here, this dog is lost. I'm going to find his owner, but you need to be nice. He's not staying here for good."

Diggory fixed his amber eyes on the dog, who'd hidden behind my legs for safety. A tense moment passed before my brown hairy monster shuffled out of the door and went to sniff the stranger. The other dog dodged the greeting, and a game of chase began around my legs.

"Enough!" I said, thoroughly peeved by the nonsense that was taking place around me. I walked into the house. After a moment, both of the dogs following me in - albeit a little sheepishly.

I got out water and then, after Diggory did some more complaining, I gave them both a treat and some food. Then, ignoring Diggory's further complaints, I called the number again. Diggory was friendly enough to the dogs we met outside of the house, but I could definitely see he was not a dog who wanted to share his home. The sooner this newcomer was reunited with his owners the better.

This time someone answered.

"Hello, I think I've found your dog," I said and then explained how I'd come home to find him sitting on my doorstep.

"Thank goodness! I took him off the lead when we were out walking but he ran off after a group of deer. The last I saw him he'd chased them over a road. My fitness is somewhat lacking… I had to give up pursuit at that point," the man on the other end of the line recounted.

I frowned. There was something familiar about this man's voice. "Might I know who I'm speaking to?"

"Oh, sure! Fergus Robinson."

I very nearly hung up.

"Fergus… is this some kind of set up?" I asked, gritting my teeth in annoyance.

There was a pause, during which I could practically hear the cogs turning in his brain. "Is that Diana Flowers? Well, well! My dog certainly has good taste. As it's you, I don't mind saying we were actually out to investigate the possibility of some mutations in the flora and fauna caused by ley lines interacting with power lines to dramatic effect. The rest is true. Barkimedes loves to chase things. I left all of my samples behind and everything."

"At least your dog is okay," I said, hoping to remind Fergus that there were more important things than ley lines and mutations.

"I'm very glad of it. I'll be over to pick him up in five. You could put the kettle on." And with that final cheek, he hung up.

"Well! You're far better mannered than your owner is," I told Barkimedes. "However, I do wish you hadn't picked my house." I still wasn't completely convinced that it had been pure chance that had led the lost dog to my house in particular. Fergus may have simply been looking for a reason to return to my property, and with the police still theoretically investigating the murder of Troy Wayland in our small neighbourhood, he probably didn't want to be caught trespassing.

The doorbell rang three minutes later. I added a point in favour for Fergus having manipulated this whole thing.

"Here's your dog," I said opening the door and gesturing to the white and brown animal. Barkimedes looked shamefaced and wagged his tail a little apprehensively before walking over to his owner with an apology written on his doggy features. I would have been impressed, had I not been fully aware that a dog would look apologetic if you trod on its foot and it was entirely your own fault. They could be naughty at times, but dogs definitely had an unrestricted kindness we humans often lacked.

"No tea and biscuits?" Fergus looked past me with hope in his expression.

"There's jelly and ice-cream if you walk down the lane and go into the first house on the left. I'm sure they'd be happy to have you."

Fergus pouted. "Come on, why so unwelcoming? It's not very British of you." I stayed silent. "I see... you think I left my dog here in order to give myself an excuse to come round and visit. That's a little presumptuous of you, isn't it?" He winked.

I wanted to punch him.

"I think you left your dog here in order to give yourself the perfect excuse to come round and visit the land that this place is built on... and probably have a good snoop around." I wasn't falling for his game of implications.

Fergus laughed and looked delighted. "That's some theory! But surely I'd just knock on your door if I wanted to do that? We're old buddies now, aren't we? We bonded over a murder at a wedding."

"You tell me. You're the conspiracy theorist," I countered. Something about this conversation was getting me all huffy. I was used to arguing against logic, but Fergus' style of debate was something that eluded me.

"I guess there are some who would call me that, but I'm the one who tries to prove or disprove theories. I'm not an expert at concocting them. But you seem to be..."

I very nearly shut the door in his smug face. The only thing that stopped me was that I'd decided I quite liked Barkimedes. He was quite well mannered, and once he'd stopped being nervous around Diggory, and Diggory had stopped being an ass, the pair seemed to get on pretty well. "Come in then," I said, defeated.

"Breakfast tea with a dash of milk and with unrefined sugar, if you have it," Fergus said, walking right by me and settling down on the sofa. "Hey, this is nice! Kind of looks like a dump on the outside. No offence." He grinned at me.

"Would that be soy milk or regular for his Lordship?" I said, sniping to regain some ground.

"Soy's bad for you. Do you know about the hormones that are in it? Or at least... are supposed to be in it. I still need to do more research on that. Cow's milk isn't perfect either but... at least it tastes good. Unlike soy."

I opened my mouth and shut it again. There was a wealth of information I could offer on both of those arguments, but I had a feeling that if I started now, I'd probably end up losing the entire day... and at the end of it, Fergus would probably still believe whatever he wanted to believe. Instead, I gritted my teeth and put the kettle on.

Fergus lounged back on the sofa. "You'll have heard that the guy at the funeral was poisoned by cyanide. It's like something out of a novel! Isn't that stuff really hard to come by?"

I paused to let the tea brew for a few moments. "It is actually possible to make it yourself. You can look the recipe up on the internet. You could do it using apricot kernels. They contain amygdalin, which can be metabolised into hydrogen cyanide - although, that would be the gaseous form of the poison. It's probably more likely that the killer made potassium cyanide, or sodium cyanide - perhaps using a pigment called Prussian blue. You've probably heard of the colour. It can be converted into potassium ferrocyanide and then reduced using sodium as an alkali metal. However, while these chemical processes are readily available to find out about - they're just simple chemical equations after all - something of the purity that I assume killed Troy Wayland fast enough that he'd barely started that cigarette would require a great understanding of chemistry and access to a lab better than the ones they have in schools. A professional laboratory," I said, thinking of the one I'd worked at locally. "Or failing that, one designed specially for tasks like this. A person with the right contacts could probably just buy the crystals. That would be easiest."

Fergus looked amused. "You should be suspect number one with knowledge like that. I reckon you're right and they just bought the stuff. That's the culture we live in these days. Why do anything yourself if you can just pay someone and have it done right? Someone planned the murder in advance, and I don't think it was anything to do with the crime of passion some of the police still want to pick as the motive. The killer didn't take any chances. They just wanted the job done." For a moment Fergus was quiet. I looked back, wondering if I should be alarmed, but he just shot me another dopey sideways grin. "Anyway, I heard the police have arrested another person from the wedding party - although no one is saying who. Even so, you should probably keep your chemical thesis under your hat."

"I just hope I get paid for doing the flowers and the backup cake," I said, suddenly realising it was nice to actually have someone to talk to. Even if it was Fergus. Diggory was a great listener, but he wasn't a person. I could have chatted to some of my neighbours, but I still wasn't clued in as to who was fighting and who was allied. I didn't want my worries getting back to Laura. Not that I was utterly convinced I should be trusting the man in front of me...

"Just whip up a batch of cyanide crystals. They'll pay up in no time."

Maybe I should have been more worried about the idiotic responses rather than the trust issue. I passed him the tea, resisting the urge to throw it on him.

"Found anything more out about the deadly soil?" I asked, figuring I deserved some comedic relief.

"Still waiting on some results to come back, but everything suggests that there is a creeping doom lurking underground. It's already poisoning the people around here... and if you're not careful, you could be next. You grow flowers, right? That means you're probably up to your elbows in this stuff from morning to night. It will happen to you much faster."

"What exactly will happen?" I asked, thinking of the

murder, Jim Holmes' habit of revenge, and finally, the skeleton in my chimney.

"That's part of what I'm hoping the research will reveal. I think it probably lowers the inhibitors in your brain that keep you from acting on any violent thoughts. It's a kind of chemical reaction. Then, something that would seem small and petty to someone not under the influence of the earth could turn into something violent in this neighbourhood. Even murder." He raised his dark eyebrows suggestively.

"Right." I wasn't buying any of this for a second. It was the most unscientific rot I'd ever heard. "I suppose all of this is due to more ley lines and chem-trails?" I said, dredging up some conspiracy theorist lingo.

"I've done more research, and I believe it is far more likely to do with a water source underground and some reaction that's happening when it interacts with the soil. It may be hospitable to something organic, like a type of parasite. You'd be amazed the effect some parasites can have on peoples' actions. There could be some electro-magnetic energies at play as well. You know… people joke about ancient burial grounds being bad news, but I always say there could be something to the old stories."

I bet you do, I silently thought. However, while I didn't like the lack of logic behind Fergus' theories, I couldn't deny that there was evidence that something was going on in the neighbourhood - influenced by soil or not. I was more inclined to think it was luck of the draw. At some point, a match had been lit, which had in turn set the whole book alight. In the past, my money would have been on Jim. But this recent murder… that had surely been started by something, too. If it really was connected to the neighbourhood rather than someone Troy had had more recent dealings with, I thought that it might have been triggered by something that had occurred when Troy Wayland made his brief return to the area.

I wondered who he'd seen and spoken to prior to the wedding and how long he'd been in town. The police had mentioned he'd been out in Kingston Hill the night before the wedding with a whole crowd of other wedding goers. Had any of my neighbours been present that night, I wondered? What could Troy have done to warrant himself being a target?

There was something about his death that was still bothering me. Something I couldn't put my finger on.

"Whoops!" With a remarkable lack of skill, Fergus managed to drop his cup on the ground, shattering it. The remainder of the tea spilt everywhere.

I wordlessly rose and went to fetch the dustpan and brush. Diggory was clumsy, too, so I was used to tidying up.

"Sorry about that! I'll buy you a new one, I promise," Fergus said, ineffectively trying to kick the pieces into a pile whilst the dogs rushed around, dangerously close to the shattered china.

"Just keep the dogs clear, please," I instructed as I swept up. "And if you think breaking a cup and offering to get a replacement is a good excuse to come back round here, you are mistaken."

Fergus' broad grin made a return. It was difficult to put this man down. "I can take a hint," he said with a wink. I privately thought he'd just taken my hint the opposite way to what had been intended.

I finished clearing up the mug and then looked at him. "Shouldn't you be going back to collect those samples of mutated flora and fauna you abandoned when Barkimedes went missing?"

Fergus raised a hand to his heart. "She remembers! I'm touched you care so much about my work. It means a lot.

You know... you should come with me on some of these investigations. I bet you'd find it interesting. It would be good to get a scientist's point of view, too."

I raised my eyebrows. "I'm not sure that you'd want to hear it."

"But I would! I want to believe in these things, but I also want them to be true. I want to see proof just as much as I think you do."

I ran a hand through my auburn hair. In spite of my annoyance and not being able to have a constructive argument with this man, there was something charming about him. Something I found myself drawn to. I decided it was his passion for what he did. It was magnetic. I understood passion like that because I had it myself for my own choice of career.

"Perhaps when my business is more on track and less off the rails," I said with a small smile.

"How is it going? You're just starting out then?" Fergus looked genuinely interested.

I found myself sitting down opposite him and then telling him the whole story - of how I'd discovered I liked flowers and felt like I was wasting my life as a cog in a machine, to how I'd inherited the property... and then everything that had happened after it. Well - almost everything. I did skip one significant discovery in particular. When I'd finished, I felt like a weight had been lifted off my chest. Although I'd shared bits and bobs about my cut flower business with various customers and neighbours, I'd never really spoken at great length with anyone. At the start, I'd kept quiet because I hadn't wanted to be shot down and have my confidence and hopes crushed. More recently, I'd simply been too busy and out of contact with everyone - apart from the occasional neighbourly chat. I was grafting hard to make this work and if it didn't... I wasn't sure what I'd do.

"I keep telling myself I can just go back to working at the chemistry laboratory if it all goes wrong. It's not exactly a competitive industry. But the thought of that is almost too much to bear."

Fergus nodded along like he understood all too well. "It's tough when you stop being a part of the machine in a world that's geared towards feeding it. For what it's worth, and I do know absolutely nothing about flowers, you look like you're doing a great job! I definitely saw some flowers flowering when I was trespassing on your land. I'm guessing that's what they're supposed to do." He grinned and I nearly laughed.

"Keep everything crossed for me," I said, thinking that he'd be one of only a couple of people who understood my vision. When my mother had returned from her cruise and discovered I'd been left a house in the expensive South East property area she'd been thrilled. When I'd told her that I wasn't selling it and that I was quitting my job... she'd stopped being thrilled. I was still in the doghouse. My mum was refusing to come round to visit, in spite of her just living a little over a mile away. Being a dutiful daughter, I'd dropped round to see her but had run every time she'd shifted the conversation onto when I was going to stop fooling around and return to my old job. My visits had been short.

I wished Fergus and Barkimedes goodbye with the strange feeling that we'd become friends. I still thought Fergus needed to take a long hard look at some of his theories, but there was something about the man that I liked. I thought that deep down, beneath all of the crazy, he was a good man.

All the same, I breathed a sigh of relief when he'd gone. While I didn't believe his theories for a second, whenever someone was in the house it felt like the skeleton in the chimney alcove was practically screaming out to be discovered. I half expected the darn thing to put itself together and wander down the stairs. I felt like a murderer covering up their crime. I wondered how Jim had dealt with covering it up for all of these years.

I shut my eyes and thought about the man who'd left me the house. I remembered his red bulgy nose and his eyes that had narrowed with cunning whenever someone crossed him. I also remembered all of the times he'd helped me out with advice when my flowers had faltered and my chemistry knowledge hadn't been enough to know that the exact hybrid I'd picked up didn't grow well outside of a greenhouse, or that this plant took its sweet time in flowering and I shouldn't expect anything from it in its first season… so maybe try something else. Jim had stuck his nose into other people's business at the allotments. He'd had an opinion on everything, and if someone had done him wrong, he'd paid them back in kind. I didn't believe he was a monster, but he'd sure as heck been good at holding a grudge. I bit my lip, remembering something else about Jim… something that could explain both his keeping of the skeleton and my own bequest of the house. He'd had a dark sense of humour. Perhaps even now he was laughing at me as I tried to figure out this mess.

The day had turned into rain. I didn't need to bother with the outside watering today. I had a little time and considered returning to my perusal of the journals. In the end, I gave it up as a waste of time. There was plenty of interest in the journals, but I didn't want to go through them hunting for a clue that probably didn't exist. I wanted to read them at my leisure and make a note of anything and everything that could help me in my business.

I decided to leave it. Instead, I found myself clipping a lead on Diggory and persuading him out of the door for a slightly wet walk in the early July rain. I shut the door and ruffled my reluctant canine's head. I'd asked the vet about his unwillingness to do, well... anything that involved physical exercise. I'd been concerned that there was something wrong with my dog. Mr Hemingway, the local vet, had examined him and announced that there was absolutely nothing wrong, he was just enjoying the easy life. The vet had empathised, saying Diggory was probably just glad to be out of having to fend for himself. I'd shot my dog a look that had let him know I knew he was milking it for all it was worth.

These days, I used a treat to get him out of the door and told him we both needed the exercise. That much at least was true. Planting always made my back ache and worked my arms, but it was hardly cardio - and staying healthy was more important than ever to me. I was running my own business and if I was sick, I wouldn't get paid.

"We'll walk down the road to the woods. Maybe the soil isn't full of impending doom down there," I said to my already sulking dog. He didn't like the rain.

I tugged on the lead a little and looked up for the first time.

Spencer had just finished putting the bins out across the road. We made eye contact. For the briefest of moments, I was transported back to being a teenager in love with the sight of him. I remembered moments just like this one when, in my imagination, we'd seemed to connect. And then we'd finally been together for that short and wonderful time... In the blink of an eye, I was thrown free of the memory and found we were both adults, living our separate lives. I raised a hand and waved hello, finding it easy to smile at him. He waved his own in return, inclining his head towards me. And then he turned and walked back into his house. I continued out along my path and down the lane. Just like two normal adults.

As the rain fell and I encouraged Diggory to stop dragging his heels, I felt the smallest of smiles tug at my lips. Whatever it was that I'd been holding onto when it came to Spencer Byrne had finally relinquished its hold. I was no longer a slightly obsessed teenager. I was a grown woman who understood that we simply weren't right for each other - no matter what teenage Diana might have imagined.

I was also able to shuck off the dark feelings of jealousy that had grown from seeing him happily married to a woman I'd unfairly judged based on our school days. I understood now that it stemmed from my own insecurity at being abandoned by a man I'd loved and trusted and had thought the world of. But in the end, I knew I would one day want to thank my ex. If I hadn't been so cruelly dumped, I'd never have left my job in London. Plus, I had my whole life to find someone who believed in me and everything I wanted to do. I didn't need to rush out and get married and start a family right this second. One day, I hoped to find someone just like that, but until then, I was doing just fine on my own.

The rain fell down and I felt a second weight lift from my shoulders. At this rate, I'd be levitating by this evening.

Now that would be something to show Fergus.

Samara was waiting on my doorstep when I arrived home from my rather soggy dog walk.

Diggory shot me an enquiring look. I shrugged slightly at him. I had no idea why the editor of the local paper was here to see me, but judging by the look on her face, it wasn't to talk about anything good.

"Hi Samara!" I said as brightly as I could manage. The woman on the doorstep looked me up and down. I knew I probably resembled a drowned rat but for whatever reason, the dark expression on her face seemed to lighten.

Oh.

This was to do with Jay.

"Might I have a word with you in private?" Samara asked, her smile full of sharp teeth.

"Sure! Come right on in. It's too wet to hang around outside." I kept my voice cheery knowing it was better to feign complete ignorance, if I wanted to get out of this one alive. Hang on... I didn't mean that literally, did I?

I swallowed down my thoughts about murder and the wisdom of letting one of my neighbours into my house. It would be fine. *Probably.*

We stepped through into my hallway together. I remained dripping slightly on the doormat with a soggy Diggory next to me. The wood floor would need wiping when Samara was gone, but I was hoping my soggy state would encourage my not entirely wanted visitor to get on with it.

"I wanted to talk to you about Jay," Samara said, thankfully biting the bullet right away.

I merely nodded encouragingly, wanting her to get it all out in the open.

"We are in a relationship. We've actually been together for a couple of years, but we've been keeping things very private. You know what our neighbours are like... they love any chance for a gossip!" She raised her eyebrows. I smiled weakly. "It's also complicated because of Lena, of course."

She bit her lip, clearly wondering how to tell me to back the heck off her man. I wasn't going to make it any easier for her. I'd done absolutely nothing wrong and had never shown any interest in her partner.

"I think Jay likes you," she said, meaning it in the friendly way.

I nodded. "He seems like a nice man. It was a pleasure

making that bouquet he commissioned for his daughter." *Ha!* There... I'd thrown her a bone about how it was all just business between us. Which it was! I had zero desire to move in on her relationship. I had enough things to worry about without getting involved with a man who had wandering eyes - at least, this visit was pushing me to suspect exactly that.

"He is nice. He's been through so much. I'm sure you know about his fiancée Kerrie running off right before the wedding?" She shook her head at the awfulness. "Even back then I liked Jay. We could all see what kind of woman Kerrie was, but love can be blind, can't it? And I'm sure they were doing their best to stay together for Lena. Even with Kerrie running around all over town."

My eyebrows shot up. "Kerrie cheated on Jay?"

Samara nodded enthusiastically. "All the time! That woman was the village bike when she lived here. I think everyone got a ride."

"Did she ever take up with Troy Wayland?" I asked, silently wondering if Jay might have murdered his fiancée and then, when Troy had returned to town, and to his old bad ways with a different bride-to-be, it had been too much for Jay to let history repeat itself and he'd killed Troy.

Samara shot me an unpleasant look. I supposed my question hadn't been all that subtle. "I have no idea. He did used to come around here years ago. I think he took up with one of Tom and Alice's tenants back when they were renting out their little apartment. He had low, low standards. I wouldn't have put it past him... or her... the little tramp. The only decent thing that woman ever did was take a hike before she tied Jay into a loveless marriage."

Ouch! Samara wasn't pulling any punches.

"It does seem that everything has worked out for the better," I said, diplomatically.

The newspaper editor nodded vehemently. "No-one will miss either of those two. A lot of people are glad Troy Wayland bit the dust." Her tone of voice let me know loud and clear that she was one of them. I wondered if Troy had done something to her personally, or if this was simply her overprotectiveness of Jay. What lengths might Samara have gone to in order to stop the past being dredged up by Troy Wayland's return?

I was glad when she excused herself. She looked sunnier than the weather outside, which I chalked up as a victory for my own cool behaviour and unwillingness to engage on a personal level on the topic of Jay. Even so, I made a mental note to be practically frosty with him, if he ever popped round for a visit again. I cared more about not being dragged into a troubled relationship than damaging my neighbourhood relations on a friendship level.

I towelled Diggory off and then let him loose into the house. Too late I realised I should have gone first as the towel was now covered in dog hair and mud. I sighed, knowing my mind had been on other things… like double-murder.

Had Jay murdered his fiancée in a fit of rage when he'd found out about her affairs? Had he then murdered her ex-lover Troy when he'd so conveniently come back to town?

Or had Samara been the one to take out Kerrie - wanting Jay for herself. She could have wanted further revenge on Troy for sticking to his old habits and reminding Jay of the past. They did say that poison was a woman's weapon…

But how does the headless skeleton and the burglar fit in to all of this? I wondered. If either of my possibilities were true, it still didn't explain why someone had come looking for the bones after all these years… or how Jim had come to have them in the first place. And just where was that missing skull?

All I had was a bundle of ideas and nothing with which to

tie them together. I only hoped the police were better mystery-solvers.

I returned home after the Sunday morning market feeling pretty darn good about myself. I'd taken the most flowers I'd ever taken to market and I'd come back with hardly anything. My stall cost had been covered in the first ten minutes, when a lady had bought a job lot of bouquets for family she was visiting. The edible flowers had fascinated and delighted as people had discovered that they didn't actually all taste the same (something I'd very recently changed my mind on myself when I'd taste-tested my new flowers-for-food). My hand tied posies had sold out very quickly indeed, and the grander bouquets had done the same - although, I had accepted an interesting offer for one from my neighbouring stall holder when the event had drawn to a close. Even better, I'd received five different enquiries about flowers for events this summer and autumn, and I'd been completely cleared out of my brand new business cards. I was hopeful that I'd be getting some phone calls and visits to my shiny website very soon. With a bit of luck, I'd be booked-up for the summer and the mantle of stress around my neck would loosen up a bit.

I opened the bag of leftover cakes and chocolates that my neighbouring stall holder had offered in exchange for my last bouquet. As I bit into a beautiful slice of coffee-walnut cake I reflected that it had been an excellent deal.

The doorbell rang just as I took a bigger bite than I probably should have done. I shrugged at Diggory, who remained lying on the sofa, and I went to answer the door, assuming it was a special delivery.

I opened the door and nearly choked on my cake.

"Mum!" I managed in-between coughing to clear the crumbs from my throat. "Dad?!" I added when a man stepped out from where he'd been hiding in my mother's shadow.

Seeing my mother on my doorstep was a big enough surprise, but my father's presence could mean only one thing:

I was in big trouble.

8

SUSPICIOUS SOIL

"What are you both doing here?" I asked, immediately on guard. My parents had split up when I'd still been a child. Although I'd had plenty of visits to see my dad and his new wife, I couldn't remember a time when I'd seen the pair of them sharing air space for more than the brief handover. "What's happened?" I added, fearing it was something terrible.

My mother rolled her eyes and flicked her perfectly coiffed silver hair off her forehead. "Don't be so dramatic, darling. Aren't you going to invite us in?" Her eyes raked up and down my t-shirt and overalls combination. I hadn't changed out of the uniform I'd worn to the market. The overalls were dark green and had 'Diana Flowers Blooms' written across the front in fancy writing. I'd been proud of the posh brand name I'd come up with for my business. I thought it added something when I wore a uniform to events.

"Oh my gosh… you're not back together again, are you?" I said, my tongue firmly pressed into my cheek. Behind my mother I thought I saw the ghost of a smile dance across my father's face. He'd always shared my sense of humour.

"Don't be ridiculous," my mother told me, marching over to the sofa and then looking down at Diggory in clear distaste.

"Diggory... off," I advised the dog. He shot me a thoughtful look with his amber eyes and then realised I wasn't kidding. With Diggory-like slowness, he rolled off the sofa and slunk away upstairs, where I knew I'd find him passed out on my bed later.

My mother inspected the sofa for dog hairs and then sat down.

"This place looks great! I wasn't expecting this when we walked up the garden path. The way I heard it from your mother, the old man left you a dump," my father said, prudently selecting an armchair far away from my mum.

"It still needs some work. I've had the essentials done to make it functional, but as you can see from the outside, there's still a lot to do. After the summer season is over, I'll probably have more time for all of that," I said, remaining standing. "Tea? Coffee?" I offered, knowing I was trying to delay whatever hammer was going to fall.

Unfortunately, I'd already started its momentum.

"The summer season? For the flowers you're growing?" My father asked. It would have sounded like an innocent enough question, had I not spotted the look he shot at my mother immediately after saying it, checking that he'd stuck to the approved script.

I folded my arms, feeling like a teenager who'd just been caught smuggling alcohol, or fooling around with a boy. "If this is some kind of intervention, please get on with it, so I can furnish you with the facts." I'd suspected something along these lines had been brewing for months, but I'd never really expected my mother to bite the bullet in this way.

My dad chortled. "She's so like you, Jennifer."

My mum shot him a quelling look. I silently thought he was correct. It was the reason my mum and I clashed heads a lot. When we made a decision and went down a path, we stuck to it. And when that path collided with the other's... all hell broke loose.

"We're just concerned about you, Diana..." she began and then shot a look at my father. He hastily nodded.

"What are you concerned about?" I asked, as if I didn't know.

My mother hit me with a look that said as much. "This little flower thing of yours... we just don't want to see you getting into debt. When you broke up with George..."

"Don't say his name," I interjected, feeling my mouth set into a firm line. We did not speak of the ex.

"I just think you're still on the rebound. All of this is you rebelling against those old feelings." She looked at me over her stylish oblong glasses. "Take it from someone who knows what it's like."

My father shifted uncomfortably in his armchair, probably regretting agreeing to walk through the door with his ex-wife. He of all people should have expected my mother to land a few punches his way, even when they were here to target me.

"It's a proper business, Mum. Anyway, it's not going too badly. Today I made four hundred pounds profit." I didn't mention that it had been a bumper morning, but who knew? It could be more than just a coincidence.

"Four hundred pounds? And it was profit?" My dad asked, looking interested for the first time.

"Well... at the end of the year when I file taxes I'll be claiming some of my original expenses back - like for compost, fertiliser, and the seeds themselves, of course... but yes. That's all profit."

"Hey, Jennifer, that doesn't sound too bad!" my dad said.

"It sounds like you had a good morning, but that kind of money isn't coming in every day now, is it?" I should have known it would be harder to pull the wool over my mother's eyes.

"No... I can only do markets on the weekend. I hope to fill the rest of the week preparing for and supplying events with flowers. Oh, and florists! I'm already selling to one florist, and I hope to supply more," I told them. "That's how I'll always make sure I have a regular paycheque. The markets may vary, and the events are where I hope to generate most of my income, but florists need stock all through the year... and I will be a supplier." I suddenly felt a burst of positivity about my business. Everything I'd just said was the way I planned to succeed and I was starting to do it, wasn't I? Today was evidence of that.

"I think she knows what she's doing," my dad said, sitting back in the arm chair and shooting an admiring glance in the direction of my wood-burner.

"Thanks for the support, Dan," my mother said, turning back to face me. My dad dropped me a wink with his bright blue eyes behind her back. "I know you were left some money by that old man who turned out to be much nicer than everyone in the village thought, but it won't sustain you forever..."

"I know, Mum. That's why I've started a business."

"But you worked so hard to be a chemist! You're smart..." I was almost able to hear the end of her thoughts: 'too smart to be a gardener'.

"I am smart and I really love growing flowers. It's really rewarding and they're pretty!" I cleared my throat, realising that these arguments weren't working on my mother. "You'd be surprised how much application my chemistry experience has in this business. Soil types and fertilisers were, after all, some of the things the laboratory specialised in analysing. They're transferable skills."

"Well, I don't know where you get it from. None of us have ever been into gardening or starting businesses," my mother said, but she didn't look as confrontational as she had done.

"There's always got to be one black sheep in the family," I said with a smile.

"How dare you! That role is already taken," my dad interjected and then hid behind a cushion when my mother shot lasers at him from her eyes. Even twenty years of separation hadn't got him out of the doghouse for ditching my mother in favour of the waitress from a coffee shop where he'd gone to drown his miseries in caffeine. When I'd been younger, I'd believed everything my mum had said about my father being a villain who'd run off with a brainless woman half his age, but Annabelle was actually only a few years younger than my mother, and she was a nice, easy-going lady who always had a smile on her face. In later years, I'd considered that perhaps my father simply hadn't been able to cope with my mother's high standards and lack of flexibility. My mum was a wonderful, powerful woman who knew what she wanted in life, but if someone didn't agree with her, she would always endeavour to change their mind - and she wasn't afraid of using significant amounts of pressure to achieve her end. Just like she was doing right now.

"I'm sure they'd let you go back to work in the laboratory in a heartbeat," my mum said.

"I'm sure they would, and if all of this fails to work out for the best, it will remain an option." Not one I'd ever be taking, but she didn't need to know that. I was going to make this business work come hell or high water. I'd decided that much already. "You should see the flower field. I've still got two more fields to convert, but I've been doing what I can with the one field, and everything's been looking good."

"I would love to see it," my dad said, standing up and patting down his legs.

After a moment more on the sofa, my mother admitted defeat. Together, we went outside to look at the flower field.

"…and these are cornflowers. They're pretty, aren't they? They've got this great English country feel and you can even eat them, so they work brilliantly in salads!"

"I am not eating flowers in my salad," my mum said flatly.

"I'll take some, if I may? Annabelle would love them. We're trying green smoothies at the moment." My dad pulled a face.

"I think that covers everything! I've got a whole bunch of evergreens growing over there…" I pointed to the edge of the field. "They'll be my bread and butter in the winter, along with whatever I can rustle up in the polytunnels. The spring, summer, and autumn will always be the months that the business does best, but with careful planning, I think I'll still make a reasonable income through the winter. If all adheres to my forecasts, I should be in profit, in terms of offsetting the initial outlay, well…" I thought about it. "Next week." If I got paid by Laura, that was. It was another piece of information my parents didn't need to know.

"As soon as that? You've only just started, haven't you?" my father asked, looking impressed.

"Yes, technically," I admitted. Laura and Ryan's wedding had been my first big event. I'd been doing the markets ever since I had my allotment, but there had been a period after Nina's flower-stomping frenzy, and before the house ownership was settled, when I'd been unable to attend. Since growing my new flowers and doing everything I could to get by in a frugal manner, things had been going pretty well. I hadn't had to dig too deeply into the money Jim had left me and now I was close to paying back every bit that I'd invested in my business. Paying for the upkeep of the property and all of its required renovations were a different matter, but that was just life. I was willing to get on with it and pray that nothing went dramatically wrong in the meantime.

"I didn't actually have a vast initial outlay. There was some equipment to buy and all of the stock I needed to start growing, but I called in a favour to get the website and business cards designed, and I did all of the work taming this field myself." I was proud of everything I'd done.

"And you've nearly made it all back?" my father clarified before turning to my mother. "That is pretty impressive, Jen. Most starting businesses don't even break even in their first year. I should know, I'm usually the one turning them all down for loans." My dad worked in a bank in Brighton.

For a moment, my mother looked at the cornflowers with a pained expression on her face. Then she sort of deflated. "Do you really think it's going to work out? I only want what's best for you. If you're serious about this... then of course I think it's very nice."

"Thanks, Mum." I reached out for a hug and she accepted without being too grudging.

"Of course, you always jumped from fad to fad when you were a child. I hope that this isn't just a rerun of that."

"Mum! I'm 27 years old."

She gave me an unconvinced look. I should have known she'd want to have the last word.

Intervention officially over, I sent my parents home - Mum with a hastily made bouquet of orchids (she wasn't a frilly woman) and Dad with a bag of edible flowers to top their smoothies with.

"That could have gone worse," I remarked to Diggory when he sauntered up behind me as I waved them off. I'd known I was going to be in for a fight when both of my parents had deigned to spend time under the same roof together, but I thought I'd come through pretty well. "All of the preparation sold it to them. Now all I've got to do is make it really successful… and before winter comes." I bit my lip. I'd definitely downplayed the income drop I was expecting come winter. There was also another pretty big unknown I hadn't been able to factor into my neat little plan, and that was the big unknown itself - the weather. Winter could come early, or it could come late. it could be long, or short. Year on year, the success of a plant could differ a lot due to the weather. You had to be half-scientist half-sooth-sayer to figure out the patterns and know what to look for. I was only in my second year of flower growing and I knew I was woefully underprepared when it came to recognising these signs. All I could do was hope that conditions were favourable. Beyond that, there was always the fear of a blight. Disease could strike at any time, and although I was always on the lookout for any signs of it amongst my plants, it was a constant concern. You could be the best business person in the world, but an act of God could ruin everything.

My dog leant against my leg - his subtle way of letting me know it was dinner time. I shook the gloomy thoughts from my head and went back inside, only to discover we'd run out of dog food. I questioned how it had happened for a moment before remembering I'd had to give some to Barkimedes yesterday, when Diggory had wanted his dinner before Fergus had turned up.

"Sorry, Diggory. Dinner's going to be a little late," I said, before asking him if he wanted to come into Merryfield with me to pick up a bag from the supermarket. My dog turned his back on me and went to sulk on the sofa.

"So much for 'man's best friend'," I muttered before leaving him to his grump.

Merryfield was pretty in the late afternoon sunshine. This quaint English village, nestled in a valley in the South East of England, was where I'd grown up, and where I had found myself returning once my London job and city life had imploded. Before I'd come back, I'd never really thought much on the idea of Merryfield being my home. There was so much about the villagers that struck me as nonsensical, and I'd also wondered about the wisdom of spending your whole life in such a tight-knit community.

However, when I'd come back, it had felt like everything was starting to slot into place again. At first, I'd been healing from my emotional wounds sustained in my old job. Then, I'd taken a chance and had discovered what I now knew was my true passion in life. I knew that I hadn't found this reason-to-be as quickly as most people did, but I knew that unlike most, I had been willing to risk everything to make it work.

From time to time I wondered where I'd be if Jim hadn't left me his property and land and the money. I thought I'd probably still be working at the laboratory for now, but I would have expanded my allotment, possibly leasing another patch, or even renting an even larger piece of land somewhere else. I would have worked on my flower growing business as a side hustle, and then a day would have come when I'd have left the laboratory anyway. Life had definitely handed me a shortcut, but it was a path I'd been determined to walk, no matter what.

I walked down the high-street I'd known since a child and reflected that although a lot had changed in my life, things in Merryfield always seemed to remain the same. *Or at least, they had seemed to,* I thought, when the board outside of the little newsagents caught my eye. Fergus had mentioned that someone had been arrested in the Troy Wayland murder investigation, but it was certainly startling to see the maid of honour's name printed on the front of the paper.

My Maid of Honour Ordeal: Arrested for Murder!

I walked over and glanced at the page, only to be shocked for a second time. Eleanor had indeed been arrested as a suspect, but she'd since been released due to an alibi that had later come to light. Eleanor was another long-time local resident I remembered from my Kingston Hill Community College days. She'd always struck me as a little bit crazed, if truth be told, but I found it hard to imagine her killing anyone.

I stopped scanning the article which listed all of the horrible things that had happened to her in custody, like being served toast and baked beans instead of a full-English breakfast. I wondered what evidence had led the police to put her under arrest. Just before I was going to walk away, my eye was caught by the final paragraph, presumably added after Eleanor had completed her rant.

A police spokesperson informed The Kingston Hill Times that Ms Feld was put under arrest for disorderly behaviour when being questioned in a murder investigation. She was held for further questioning when a monetary debt owed to her by the deceased that resulted in a court case came to light, but was later released without charge.

So that was the real story. Eleanor Feld had probably flipped out at the police questioning her and got herself arrested. She had never been a real murder suspect at all. The only hint that there was any basis in her involvement in the murder was the debt that the spokesperson had mentioned. In my head, I'd concocted some sort of idea that Eleanor might have been nuts enough to want to ruin Laura's wedding - despite her being picked as the maid of honour. It would be in keeping with Eleanor's unpredictable character. This debt was interesting, too. I wondered how much Troy had owed Eleanor and why? Even so, I was close to certain that she wasn't the killer as soon as I thought about the way Troy had died. It had been planned and precise. Clinical, even. Eleanor was practically the opposite of that definition.

I turned and continued to walk down the street, only to bump into a familiar face.

"Lauren! What are you doing here?" I asked, delighted to see my old school friend. Lauren had started working in London fresh out of university, just as I had. She'd studied law and had been employed by a firm who worked on patents and copyrights the last I had heard.

"Diana! It's been ages. How are you? What are you doing back in Merryfield?" she echoed.

We exchanged more astonished pleasantries before Lauren suggested we pop into the coffee shop, if we both weren't busy. I spared a thought for Diggory sitting at home waiting for his food and decided he could wait a little longer. He was a bottomless pit who could probably do with more time between meals. I fully expected there to be some sign of his wrath when I returned home, but I factored that in and still decided to say yes.

Two minutes later, we were settled in The Merry House Cafe with a couple of lattes.

"How's the job?" I asked, curious to discover if Lauren was enjoying her career.

She waved a hand. "Terrible most days, but it pays the bills, you know?" She said it like it was just a fact of life.

I bit my tongue to keep from asking why she didn't try to do something else. It was the kind of decision you had to make on your own.

"How about you? Still working in London?" she asked.

"No, I quit that job a long time ago. I was working in a local laboratory, but I recently quit."

Lauren's fair eyebrows shot up. "Oh? What are you doing instead?"

"I grow flowers. I supply florists (well... florist at the moment, but that would change soon!) and flowers for events and so on."

"Lucky you! That sounds like a dream. So... you're just doing that?"

I nodded, knowing exactly what she was getting at. "It's what I should have been doing all along... I just didn't know it." I looked up over my latte and wasn't unsurprised to discover that Lauren didn't look convinced. "What brings you back to Merryfield?" I asked, deciding a change of topic would be best.

"I'm actually dating someone we used to go to school with. It's the weirdest thing... I saw him on the underground in London and decided to say hello. We got chatting and met up for a drink, and the next thing I knew, it turned into an actual relationship." She shook her head. "Teenage me would be over the moon to know that she gets the cute guy from secondary school all of these years later."

"Oh come on... who is it?" I asked, feeling just like the teenager Lauren was talking about.

"You remember the guy I used to spend all of our maths classes staring at?"

"Joe Cogger?" I remembered a guy with dark, slightly

curling short hair and a sideways smile that had rendered him kind of cute.

"Yeah! That's the one. It's funny... you think you've left your old life behind once you've gone to university and moved away to start a new job, but just like that, you find yourself back in Merryfield and back where you started." She looked thoughtful for a moment.

"Something definitely pulls us back to where we come from," I acknowledged, knowing it had certainly been the case for me. When I'd quit my London job I could have ended up anywhere. It was luck, or perhaps fate, that had seen me stationed at a laboratory so very close to my home-town. I thought Lauren had experienced the same thing. "What's Joe doing these days?" I asked, figuring it must be something local.

"He manages a pub just outside Kingston Hill, but he's renting a flat in Merryfield. I think it's so he can check on his mum more often. She's not doing too well." Lauren looked solemn for a second before brightening again. "Whereabouts are you living these days?"

"I'm over in Little Larchley."

Lauren goggled. "Is there something I don't know about selling flowers?!"

I smiled in spite of myself. "I think you'd be surprised when it comes to the market for cut flowers, but I was lucky enough to be left a house and land by Jim Holmes when he passed away."

Lauren nodded. "I heard that he died. Supposedly there was some drama around it?"

"Isn't there always drama when Merryfield folk are involved?" We exchanged a knowing look before I explained exactly what had befallen Jim Holmes.

"Little Larchley is a nice neighbourhood, isn't it? I

remember there was a guy called Jay who lived there? He had a fiancée?" Lauren rubbed her chin thoughtfully.

"Jay's still there, but his partner left him," I said, wondering how Lauren knew of the pair.

"She disappeared, didn't she?" Lauren said, surprising me with her knowledge. "My sister had some trouble with Jay. He decided to pursue her romantically... but get this - it was while he had a kid and was planning to get married! Can you believe that? Harriet initially thought he was just being friendly to her, but he really started pushing things. She told him she wasn't comfortable with being 'the other woman' in the relationship, and the next thing she knew, he was out showing someone else the beauty spots that she'd shown him when they'd gone on walks together."

"Do you know who the other person was?" I asked, immediately thinking of Samara and her longterm infatuation.

Lauren tilted her head from side to side. "I think it was someone living practically next door to Jay. Harriet found out all about her at the time. I think she was considering telling all to the fiancée. The only thing I remember is that this other woman was blonde and not a local. But can you believe that?! People talked about his fiancée leaving him like it was some big mystery why a woman would get out of that situation... I don't think there's any mystery at all. Jay wanted to start a secret relationship with my sister. I bet it was the same story with this other woman... only, I'm guessing it didn't stay secret." She raised her eyebrows at me.

I nodded in agreement. Inside, I mentally added another possibility. What if this non-local 'blonde woman' was none other than the tenant Alice and Tom had been in the process of evicting? It certainly wasn't someone fitting Samara's description. The tenant might have threatened to tell Kerrie. Jay could have killed her to keep her quiet... only for it to all come out anyway. There was even a chance that Kerrie may have done the killing and then done a runner... although that didn't make as much sense when it came to Troy's murder. *Unless his death was a professional hit commissioned by someone he angered in London,* I silently allowed. There was still a chance that these murders weren't connected at all. The only thing that led me to believe they were tied together was the timing of the break-ins, which coincided so neatly with Troy's return to town a couple of days before the wedding.

I had to be missing something.

"Jay and his daughter are doing well. He's seeing the local newspaper editor," I said, already knowing that the pair's 'secret' relationship was public knowledge, no matter what Samara may believe. Tom had told me himself and you'd have to be blind to not see the way the pair behaved around one another.

"Samara Henley?"

"Yes, do you know her?" I asked, curious but not unsurprised. Merryfield and its surrounding satellite villages tended to be close-knit.

"Not really. I know about the local paper, of course, but it's my mother who knew the family. When she was working in the local practice as a nurse, she told me Samara used to bring in her daughter a lot." Lauren pulled a face. "There used to be a surprising amount of drugs around locally. I guess the kid got caught up in it." She shot me a sideways look that said 'this is just between us, right?' I nodded my head in return. I wouldn't be gossiping, and as Lauren's mother had already confided it in her, the initial confidentiality lapse had happened long ago. "I think my mum said the daughter went off travelling to get away from her problems here."

I suddenly remembered Tom mentioning 'troubles' when

referring to Samara's daughter. I hadn't thought much of it at the time, but now it all made sense.

"I saw that Troy Wayland was murdered. It's about time all of it caught up with him," Lauren said, as if continuing down the same line of thought.

I shot her a surprised look.

Lauren raised her eyebrows. "Didn't you know he was the local drug dealer? A lot of people around here despised him for it. I hate to say it, but the guy had it coming."

"I'm starting to think that myself," I commented. I found myself adding yet another possible turn of events - one where Samara's daughter had never gone travelling at all and had instead met her tragic end in Little Larchley. Her distraught mother, who'd mysteriously decided to bury her child without telling anyone about her death, had then taken her shot at revenge when her daughter's enabler had made his return.

"...crazy how some people can go travelling and not come back," Lauren was saying. "I don't think I could ever just cut myself off from my parents. Mine pushed me through a lot of the university stuff, but even though I found it tedious at the time, I can see it from their point of view now. They wanted me to have a solid career. I have enough money to live on and it's secure. It makes sense, doesn't it?"

I thought about my mum and dad, who were guilty of the same faults. "I do think our parents have our best interests at heart. But I don't think they always know the right way for us. That's something you have to choose for yourself." I smiled as I thought back to the conversation I'd had with my mum and dad. After I'd demonstrated that I really had thought everything through and that this was it - this was what I wanted to do with my life - they'd given their support.

"Well… I suppose so," was all Lauren had to say to that. We chatted a little bit longer about work and life with me sharing memories from my lab work, as it was the only way we were able to relate. We made some vague noises about meeting up again in the future, but I wasn't convinced Lauren was serious. I hadn't realised it until now, but there was a wedge between me and the friends with whom I'd grown up and shared goals. Lauren had opted to stick with her conventional career, whereas I was sure she thought I'd gone completely off the rails.

I smiled as I walked down the street to visit the supermarket. I thought I was actually okay with that.

My smile dropped when I remembered the other part of our conversation. It would appear that Jay and his fiancée had been guilty of infidelity - if both Samara and Lauren had their facts straight. I wondered if Samara knew *that* little truth about the man she seemed to have put on a pedestal.

Jay and Kerrie's potential interaction with Tom and Alice's tenant was something I hadn't foreseen because I hadn't realised the timelines matched. Could it be that Jay had carried on with the tenant, only for it to go sideways in such a way that he'd ended up killing and burying her? Tom and Alice still believed she'd run off with everything she'd been able to lay her hands on when they'd been in the process of eviction... but that could have been exactly what the killer had wanted them to conclude.

Or had Kerrie been the one to get caught in the crossfire after taking up with Troy? Alternatively, had she murdered the tenant out of jealousy?

Or did the bones belong to Samara's daughter who hadn't really gone travelling? It was a mess of possibilities.

I bit my lip, wondering why - if any of those were the real turn of events - Jim had subsequently dug up the bones. If I believed Jim had dug the skeleton up soon after the body had been buried, I probably would have been okay with the idea that he'd used his knowledge to blackmail the murderous, cheating fiancée into leaving Jay and daughter without so much as a goodbye. However, the receipt in the planter disagreed with that timeline.

This whole skeleton thing was a nightmare.

Not to mention that I now had a new candidate for the skeleton's identity in the form of Samara's missing daughter.

In the end I told my speculative mind to be quiet and focused on buying Diggory's dog food.

I returned home to discover that I needed to see someone about replacing the cushions on my sofa. Other than that, the damage was minimal. After he'd eaten his dinner, I kicked Diggory out into the garden as punishment, and we both spent the rest of the evening sulking.

Disaster struck the next morning.

I was up early for my usual flower watering. Midway through giving the hardy gerberas a drink, I noticed something disturbing. There were dark spots on the leaves and the plants looked wilted. I considered the possibility that they just needed a drink, but the soil was still moist. I gave one of the gerberas an experimental poke and felt a stab of horror when half the plant collapsed onto the earth. I bent down for a closer inspection and discovered that the roots were gone. There was nothing at all keeping the plant upright below the stems sticking into the earth. The blooms on the gerberas were still bright and cheery but there was no doubt in my mind that a lot of these plants were as dead as the dodos. I stopped my inspection of the ruined flowers and walked along the row of blooms, stopping and inspecting them as I went.

The gerberas weren't the only casualties.

Here and there, my flowers were dying. The symptoms

were always the same - wilted leaves and something (surely a rot?!) that had eaten away at their roots.

I was devastated. I'd poured everything into my dream of growing and selling flowers. Now I was up against something that could decimate my plans - and at such a crucial stage! I'd been relying on a bumper summer to get me through a poorer winter. With this new development, I was already afraid that Diana Flowers Blooms wouldn't even make it through the first cold snap.

I took a few deep breaths and told myself not to panic. I was a scientist and an analyst. All I needed to do was find out what was wrong. Then I could fix it... before it ruined the rest of my summer crop. I bit my lip, thinking about how easy it had been in the old days to take in a soil sample and analyse it at the laboratory where I'd worked. I shook my worry away. I still had friends at the lab. Checking the affected plants and the soil they were in wouldn't be a problem. But before I did that, there was one other place where I could look for the answer...

"I should have done this right at the start," I muttered as I made a beeline back to the house carrying all of the flowers I'd been able to salvage from the stricken plants. They looked bright and happy - a stark contrast to what I was feeling inside. I dumped them in the sink rather unceremoniously. I would have to think of something to do with them later. For now, I stalked up the ladder into the attic to see if I could find an answer to my newest problem.

Jim's journals were jumbled for the most part, which had frustrated me the first time I'd looked through them. The only thing they did have was brightly coloured tabs that stuck out at all sides. These tabs were annotated with things like 'rhododendron, dahlia, delphinium' and so on. After a brief flip through the notes I found what I was looking for.

I turned to the page in one of the journals that carried the tab labelled 'disease'.

A bright yellow post-it note was what caught my attention first. This book was old - Jim had stopped planting flowers years ago - but the note was new. I could tell by its bright colour that was incongruous with the rest of the book.

The writing on it was also a bit of a dead giveaway.

You'll find it beneath the tea. I didn't do it. I trust that you will do the right thing.

*Why didn't **you** do the right thing?* I wondered, not feeling too fond of my benefactor in that moment. The note didn't even tell me anything I didn't already know. I'd guessed that Jim wasn't the one who'd killed the owner of the skeleton. I'd also guessed that, for whatever reason, I was supposed to do something with the bones - rather than march them straight over to the police. Or perhaps the ball was in my court as far as that went. The note implied that anyway.

"Thanks for nothing," I muttered, taking the note and rolling it into a tiny ball. I tossed it in the direction of the chimney. It bounced off the plasterboard and lay there on the floor. Then, feeling even more grumpy than I had when I'd entered the attic, I started reading the page that Jim had assumed I would read all along.

I had learned something from that note after all. Jim had known I'd come looking for information on plant diseases.

He'd known there was something wrong with the land he'd given me.

I shut my eyes for a moment thinking of everything

Fergus had been telling me and wondering if somehow, in some strange way, he'd been right all along. Was there some secret doom lurking in the soil that killed everything it touched? Was my flower business about to be destroyed by a dreadful fate?

I looked at the page.

The symptoms were all there. The wilting, the rotting, the despair. I read down, desperately hoping for the solution. Jim had written that he'd spotted these symptoms over the years and they'd been getting worse with every year of planting. He'd put down fertiliser and tried different plants with mixed levels of success. He thought it was probably the soil that was doing it, so he'd laid fresh stuff every year, but it was still a problem.

And that was it.

There was no diagnosis of the disease and no solution. As far as I could tell, it may even have been the reason that Jim had upped sticks and transferred his green fingers to an allotment in Merryfield. Not only had I been saddled with a headless skeleton, I'd been landed with suspicious soil.

"It is not going to end this way," I said to the emptiness of my attic. A shaft of light suddenly entered the dormer window, like a message from God, as the sun rose higher still in the sky. My logical mind informed me it was a coincidence, but I needed every ounce of hope I could lay hands on right now. I decided to take it as a sign I was on the right track. I could solve my problems - all of them - if I just refused to give up.

It was time to go back to the lab.

9

A SPOT OF SKULDUGGERY

I t was strange being back at the laboratory. It was even stranger being there after hours.

A phone call to my old colleague, Darrow, had been enough to secure me access to my old place of work and permission to run the soil and plant samples through their machines, as well as running several tests of my own. Ever since leaving the lab, I'd meant to invest in a microscope and a 'field kit' of my own. Darrow had made it clear that this favour was a one-off, so I'd better do some shopping soon.

I started with the microscope, looking down at the leaves I'd pulled from the affected plants and hoping to see something that would give me the blinding realisation of exactly what the problem was and how I could fix it... preferably before it wiped out my entire summer's worth of plants.

Instead, I found myself staring at a black blotch on a leaf with no clue as to what it could mean. This was where my weakness lay. I could analyse chemical solutions and components until the cows came home, but my knowledge of horticulture was significantly lacking when compared to my knowledge of chemistry. With an empty sigh, I gave up on the plant itself and instead moved on to inspect the soil. I knew what to look for in soil. I'd been examining samples for years. If there was something present that I'd missed during my initial sample analyses I'd done before I'd quit my job, I would find it. And then, using chemistry, I would fix it.

With fresh hope, I tested the soil acidity. It showed a pH value of 7.0, so heavy metals weren't the problem. It's neutral pH also meant that it wasn't an alkaline issue, so I didn't need to take a closer look at the salts.

Next, I looked down a microscope at my first sample. After adjusting the lens, I did find something.

The soil was full of what looked like worms. Microscopic worms. I watched them wiggle around and felt horror rising in me. Were these creatures responsible for my plants' vanishing roots? What the heck were these things?

In times of trouble, when my area of expertise was no help at all, I turned to Google.

"Nematodes," I concluded after some careful searching. Apparently, there were several different types of these organisms. I did my best to match the worm-like things under the microscope with the ones listed as being nibblers of roots, leaves, and stems.

I found some concerning discrepancies. The genus of nematode that matched the description of the roundworms I had under my microscope was supposed to eat away at roots and stems... but only of specific plants - mostly vegetables. I could understand why that might have driven Jim to seek fresh pastures, but nematodes shouldn't be affecting my flowers.

The disastrous extent of the damage wasn't covered in any description I could find. Root-knot nematodes were supposed to be a bit of a pain - not an apocalyptic problem that could devastate entire crops and kill plants stone dead.

They usually resulted in a few wonky, ugly carrots, and reduced crop production.

Finally, one of the suggestions on how to get rid of the darn things (in a natural way) was to plant French marigolds in abundance. I already had lots of those growing in my flower field, as they were a colourful, if small, addition to my hand-tied posies. In theory, the nematodes should have been wiped out by the presence of the marigolds. The French ones in particular worked as a trap crop. Once nematodes entered the marigolds' roots, the marigolds stopped the pests from developing further in their life cycle - or even actively killed the nematodes when they attempted to feed. But it was clear that this had not occurred.

Another suggestion was to plant rye grass, but I had a strong feeling that none of these natural methods would work, when the pests themselves seemed to defy all logic.

After searching for another solution, I found there was only one logical conclusion that could be drawn. For some reason, these nematodes, that I believed were the cause of my problem, were different. They were deadlier than the variants listed online, and they were resistant to the usual methods of dispatch. I assumed that the topsoil I'd put down at the start of the growing season had protected my plants thus far, but now the nematodes had got on top of things... and I had no way to stop them.

I shut my eyes and took several deep breaths before the answer came to me. Deirdre. She'd had an allotment close to mine, and while she was another veg specialist, she was partial to the odd flower. I reckoned she'd know a thing or two about the pests that were bothering me. Hopefully, she'd have a solution up her sleeve.

I would settle for anything short of salting and burning.

I shook my head, knowing that wasn't exactly true. As lots of my flowers were farmed for food purposes, I didn't like to use anything that wasn't natural. No harsh chemical fertilisers or pesticides were used. I'd seen their negative effects on the quality of soil under a microscope. I knew what chemicals did to the environment and the water table. But being all natural came at a cost... one I suspected I had just fallen foul of. I just hoped it didn't cost me absolutely everything.

I returned home late that night with my fears soothed. Deirdre and the rest of the Merryfield Murder Mystery Fans book club (who'd been in the middle of a meeting when I'd come banging on the door) had listened to my fears about my flowers and had all sympathised. Then the suggestions had come. Some of them had sounded crazy - like planting a few crystals in the ground to disperse the negative energy - but there were others I thought would be worth a whirl.

I left the meeting feeling full of hope and cake, and having skilfully avoided talking about the Troy Wayland murder. Somehow everyone in the club knew that I'd been the one to find the body. If I were Walter Miller, I'd be keeping a little quieter around the police station's receptionist. I'd managed to brush them off by claiming I was supposed to keep silent for legal reasons. Whilst they'd still been debating what those 'legal reasons' could be, I'd thanked them for their help and made a swift escape.

Now that I was back in my house with Diggory for company I found my shoulders losing some of the tension they'd held ever since I'd discovered the plight of my flowers. I had some solutions to try, and if that failed I also had a foolproof (albeit not ideal) plan that involved building massive raised beds with soil that stayed separate from the stuff I was currently growing in. It would be a huge undertaking. I was hopeful that it wouldn't be one I'd be forced to undertake - as it also involved a lot of risky replanting - but I'd promised myself I'd do anything to make this business work, and this task was definitely included in that remit.

"Time for some fancy tea," I told my dog. For once, he'd decided he had excess energy and was zipping around the living room. I'd opened the backdoor for him to go outside, but he seemed to prefer causing havoc in the house. I couldn't say I was too surprised. We had yet to attend puppy training classes in order for Diggory to play catchup after his false start in life, however, I had a feeling he wasn't cut out for obedience. It wasn't that Diggory lacked intelligence. One look in his eyes would tell you that he knew exactly what you were asking him to do. He just didn't want to do it. I might as well have owned a cat.

A red rubber skittle skidded across the floor and hit my foot with a squeak. I looked down at the dribble covered toy in distaste and managed to toss it out of the door into the field beyond… where the darn thing was supposed to stay. Diggory shot me a look like I'd just told him Christmas was cancelled and then stalked out of the door into the night to get his toy.

"Definitely the cattiest dog that ever did dog," I muttered, finding myself smiling as I warmed a pan of milk ready for a chai latte. As soon as it was steaming, I took it off the heat and added it to the already brewed chai tea in my glass cup. I watched as the amber liquid mixed with the milk, and then I added a teaspoon of honey. I knew that my drink wasn't really much more virtuous than a hot chocolate, but I felt that after the day I'd had, I deserved it.

"Here's to Diana Flowers Blooms… overcoming parasites and going on to prosper!" I raised my cup with a smile.

The cool night air blew through the open door, and I listened to the sounds of the nocturnal world awakening.

Wildlife rustled through the bushes and a few birds chirped their final songs of farewell to the day that had been.

As I sipped my drink, my mind turned to murder and missing persons.

The length of time the skeleton in my attic had been kicking around for bothered me. Talking to my neighbours had thrown up three potential candidates for the skeleton's identity, but I was no closer to narrowing it down, and I also didn't think it was anything I could casually drop into conversation. At least - not without arousing suspicion.

I was convinced that one, or more, of my neighbours knew what had really happened to at least one of the three potential missing persons. I was also sure that the person breaking in to all of the locals' houses was the killer. If I asked the wrong neighbour the wrong question, I could end up being the next woman to go missing from Little Larchley.

"Figure it out," I muttered into my latte. Why had Jim ended up with the skeleton? I wondered if he'd seen someone burying a body. He'd have known the location and could have later chosen to dig it up. Why had he not immediately told the police when he'd first seen the body being buried? I was unfortunately willing to concede that in this instance, Jim's character was to blame. He'd seen the opportunity to have something on one of his neighbours... neighbours he famously hadn't got along with... and he'd kept his mouth shut until...

I thought about it.

Something must have happened to inspire him to dig up the skeleton, but I had no idea what the killer might have done to deserve it. I did, however, think it had been Jim's way of wreaking revenge, and I was willing to bet he'd left the skull behind deliberately - just to make the culprit sweat. I knew Jim had been no stranger to that kind of ruthless behaviour. When he'd believed other vegetable growers on the allotment were sabotaging his prized plants, he'd wasted no time in hatching nefarious plans of his own. I'd seen warfare on the Merryfield allotments, and I was certain that he'd formed the habit long before his allotment days.

I frowned, feeling a headache come on as I focused everything I could on the mystery of the skeleton and the unanswered questions. Why had the break-ins started so recently? The multiple burglaries suggested to me that the killer wasn't sure which of their neighbours had the skeleton. As to why the searching had begun now... I could only hypothesise that something had caused the killer to act. Either they'd discovered for the first time that the skeleton was gone, or something had happened to make them fear that their crime was going to come to light. I remembered the shattered ribs and saw it as a stark reminder that, while this crime was old, the killer was brutal.

Next question... how exactly had Jim seen one of his neighbours burying a body? Even if you were out in the fields, my neighbours' gardens were mostly surrounded by high hedges that kept privacy pretty well. Jim would either have had to be right up against the hedge peeping over the top, or pressed up against a thin patch. Whilst I knew that most Merryfield residents had a shared love of gossip and sticking their noses into other's business, I couldn't imagine Jim wasting his time on spying.

"Of course! The journals!" I said. When I'd moved in, I'd been told the journals were in the attic. I'd also found a chair and table up there. At the time, I'd assumed they were just there for storage, but now I suspected that Jim might have used the attic as his journal-writing office - the same way I ran my business from that desk. And I knew from personal experience that you could see the whole neighbourhood from the windows up there.

"Darn it," I said, knowing that the view didn't narrow

down my options. Every house was visible. The only member of the hamlet I didn't have a bird's eye view of was Mrs Bellefleur. I knew she didn't leave her house these days, so I was skeptical that she was the one running around breaking into people's houses searching for the bag of bones.

I was at another dead end.

I was draining the dregs of my latte when all hell broke loose outside.

"Diggory!" I said, suddenly remembering I'd last seen the dog running into the garden to fetch the toy I'd thrown through the door.

I rushed out into the night to find out what was making that unearthly wailing.

My eyes adjusted to the darkness as I ran across the field calling for Diggory. I heard him bark in the distance and crossed the first field and the second in search of him. Eventually, I saw his shadow over by the sycamore tree that hung over Jay's house. When I got closer, I was able to see what was causing the horrible wailing.

There was a cat in the tree.

Diggory had his front paws up against the trunk. He was staring up into the branches, looking very pleased with himself. He'd obviously chased the poor cat up there. I felt my shoulders sag with relief. For one horrible moment, I'd feared that someone was being murdered.

"Come on, Diggory. Let's come away so the poor thing can climb back down." As I was tugging him back by his collar, light suddenly flooded out of the house over the hedge. I heard the sound of someone running across the lawn.

"Kipper! Kipper!" Jay called, probably having heard the death wails.

"Your cat's up a tree. I'm really sorry. I let Diggory out in the garden and didn't think anything of it."

"Is Kipper okay?" Jay asked.

I looked up into the branches. Yellow eyes and flat ears confronted me. Kipper didn't look too cuddly, but he looked fine to me. "He's okay. If I take Diggory away, I'm sure he'll come back down."

"Poor Kipper. He's only just started to go outside again since what happened the last time. I suppose he won't want to go out again after this." Jay sounded morose.

"What happened last time?"

"It was Jim. Kipper used to be the kind of cat who liked to roam around. Occasionally Kipper might have used Jim's freshly dug vegetable beds to do his business in. Who can blame him for picking them over hard earth? But Jim really took offence to that. He installed sprinklers that turned on when a motion sensor was triggered. It gave the postman quite a shock." I didn't know whether to laugh or look serious. "But it did work on Kipper. The poor animal was so traumatised by constantly being sprayed whilst he went about his business, he got too scared to go out. It's only recently he's decided it might be okay to wander again. Almost as if he sensed that the old man was gone for good." Jay sighed. "I suppose I should just put a really high fence around our garden, but that will ruin the country view."

"I'm sure there's no need for that. We could just message each other when our animals are out and about." I was making a big concession. One of the great things about having land was being able to let Diggory run all over it without worrying about his safety, but I did empathise with the cat's plight.

"No, I wouldn't want to inconvenience you." There was something stiff about the way Jay said it. I was suddenly reminded of the way I'd left the birthday party as quickly as possible and the little chat I'd had with Samara. Behind Jay's garden hedge I rolled my eyes. I hadn't wanted to get involved with his relationship with Samara. I was not going to be involved with some ridiculous neighbourhood love triangle that could end very nastily - especially if one of the people involved had a track record of taking out the opposition in a very final manner. History was not going to repeat itself.

"Let me know if there's anything more I can do. Goodnight," I said, leading Diggory away by his collar. When he resisted that, I rustled a hand in my pocket, finding a dog treat there. Diggory quickly decided that treats trumped chasing cats.

I gave Diggory the treat when we were back inside and shut the door after him with a sigh. So much for there being an end to the neighbourhood feuds now that Jim was gone. I suspected I may have just opened a fresh can of worms.

"But it is my land, and I can't help it if Diggory likes chasing things," I muttered and then realised Jim himself had probably used similar arguments. There had to be give and take in any relationship, and it seemed to me that no one around here wanted to give.

"It's the minerals in the soil," I said, lapsing back to joking about Fergus' theories, before remembering that there was in fact something wrong with the land. I frowned. With a bit of luck, he'd never find out the truth. I wasn't sure I'd ever be able to live it down.

My doorbell rang the next morning, but I was already out in the field taking action against the nematode scourge. "Come round into the field!" I called. A moment later there was the sound of the gate opening. Diggory ran across to greet the visitor.

I shook my hands free of soil and turned to see who it

was. Fergus Robinson was striding across the field towards me.

"So much for him never finding out the truth," I muttered, ready to face up to a lot of unjustified 'I told you so's'.

"Morning! I was in the neighbourhood and thought I'd drop in to see how you are. You can't be too careful when you're living on land that's as bad as what you've got here," Fergus greeted me cheerily.

I did my best to take a subtle sidestep to the left in order to cover up the big bag of organic matter I was hoping to mix into as much of the loose soil around the plants as I could. I'd also upped the watering cycle, as dry plants were apparently more susceptible to nematode attack. After the conversations I'd had last night about what action to take, I'd done further research and had made the unfortunate discovery that moving my currently-surviving plants to raised beds risked bringing the mysteriously deadly nematodes right along with them.

This morning I'd made the decision to hack down as many of the weeds and shrubs as possible in field number two and start building the raised beds. I'd then plant them up as quickly as possible with fast growing blooms and hope it would be enough to see me through a strong summer and autumn season - in spite of the late planting. I had a lot of labour ahead of me, but I was desperately hoping it would pay off.

"It's nice to see you, too," I said, finding that I meant it. Since our last meeting, the conspiracy theorist had grown on me. "Did you hear that they released the maid of honour? From the newspaper report it sounded like she didn't have much to do with the murder at all. There were some questions about a debt that Troy owed her, but I think she was arrested for being difficult in questioning." I hesitated. "Not that I can blame her if Walter Miller was the one doing the asking."

"That's actually why I thought I'd come round to see you. I heard on the grapevine that the police are looking for a new suspect. I wondered if they'd been back in the neighbourhood asking questions?"

I shook my head. "I haven't seen or heard anything. Wasn't everyone sold on the idea of Troy being killed by someone from the city?"

Fergus shrugged. "The efficiency of the method of dispatch would fit with some criminal gangs' modus operandi, but strange that it was done way out here in the sticks, don't you think? Rather inconvenient for an assassin."

"Perhaps they knew Troy would have his guard down."

"Perhaps. Or perhaps…" Fergus started to say but he was interrupted by someone shouting 'hello!' very loudly.

We both turned towards the sound and discovered someone was calling from the opposite side of the hedge. I walked along until the hedge got a little lower. It could probably do with a trim, I reflected, mentally adding it to my less urgent 'to do' list.

"How are you, Tom?" I said, smiling at the writer. He smiled back, two dimples appearing in his cheeks. I was struck again by how attractive he was. There was something carefree about his mannerisms and happiness, and when you paired it with that chiselled jaw and his naturally sporty physique (I'd seen him jogging up and down the lane) I could see why Alice might be willing to put up with some of his faults.

"I am very well, thank you." Tom turned his megawatt smile onto Fergus, who looked amusingly nonplussed by the man's friendliness. "Don't I know you from the wedding?"

"Yes, I was the stand-in best man. I know Ryan from our university days. Fergus," my companion said, extending a hand over the top of the hedge. I tried not to laugh as the two men tried to reach and shake hands and ended up nearly falling face-first into the prickly hawthorn.

"Diana, I wanted to ask if you'd like to come to a party we're throwing. It's nothing fancy - just a little barbecue to celebrate summer getting into its swing, you know? We invite all of our neighbours every year. It usually keeps us in gossip until the next summer." He winked at me. "With that unfortunate murder still unsolved I bet that's all anyone will be talking about." He shook his head, either lamenting the horrible crime or the lack of new gossip. I wasn't sure which.

"Aren't you worried that one of your neighbours might slip some more of that cyanide into the barbecue chicken?" Fergus joked, saying what I was thinking, but would never have voiced. I shot him a disapproving look, but there was something about his charm that let him get away with making outrageous comments. I was starting to wonder if Fergus portrayed himself as a kookie conspiracy guy precisely so he could get away with murder. Well, not literal murder.

At least… I hoped not.

For a second I considered Fergus' vague 'security service' history. Might he be perfectly placed to source the cyanide crystals used in the murder?

"I didn't do it, you muppet," Fergus said out of the corner of his mouth.

I wiped my expression. Was I really so transparent?

Tom's smile faltered for a second as he watched this pass between us without hearing it or understanding. "I heard that Troy had a lot of gambling debts. I reckon someone got tired of waiting for him to pay up," Tom said, as if that settled the whole matter.

I shook my head. "But that's idiotic. If you murder him, he'll never pay. Some form of torture would be far more effective." I realised what I'd said and shut my eyes. The Merryfield Murder Mystery Fans' chatting had clearly got under my skin.

"Anyone could have killed him," Fergus said with an easy grin, covering for me.

"Yes, exactly," Tom replied, pleased to be back on track with our lighthearted speculative conversation. "So, will you come to the party this weekend? You can bring a guest if you'd like." His eyes not so subtly danced across to Fergus and then back to me. I felt my cheeks warm. "I invited the new neighbours, too. It will be good to meet them both! I hear they're about to have a baby?"

I felt my stomach drop, even though I'd convinced myself I was over Spencer and his new wife. "They are," I confirmed, forcing a smile. "I've known them both since our school days. I'm sure they'll fit in perfectly," I said, hoping for something neutral to say, before our conversations about murder and neighbourhood feuds popped back into my head. Perhaps it hadn't been a tactful choice of words after all.

"I'm sure they will," Tom said, smoothing the whole thing over. "Shall I tell Alice you're both coming?"

It took me a second to realise he was talking about Fergus.

I looked across at the conspiracy theorist with a startled expression.

"We're looking forward to it," Fergus said with a wide smile, casually laying an arm across my shoulders.

Tom's eyebrows lifted a fraction. "Great! I will see you both on Sunday." And with that, he disappeared back behind the hedge.

I turned to find Fergus grinning at me. "Do you think that will set the neighbourhood tongues wagging?"

I threw my hands up in the air and stalked off. I did not have time for this nonsense.

"Come on, it'll be fun. We'll be able to look for Troy's killer. I didn't buy that whole gambling debt theory either. I guess we shouldn't be surprised that he owed money to more than just the maid of honour. You were right to point it out."

"Or stupid to point it out to people who could be involved."

It took Fergus a second to realise what I was implying. "Do you really think I might have done it? With my secret conspiracy theory contacts, right?" He was grinning again.

I shrugged, wondering if I'd ever get back to my stricken flowers.

"Fortunately for us both, I have an alibi. The morning before the wedding I was investigating crop circles near Blackberry Farm. I have the selfies to prove it, too. You wanna see?"

I considered. "You know what? I think I'll just take your word for it."

I bumped into Samara the next morning when I was on my way out. The lane outside my house was teeming with activity. Spencer and Francesca had hired a group of builders to do something or other to their new property. Judging by the large wooden beams that were being carried around, it was something serious. I wondered if they'd got proper planning permission… before I decided to keep my mouth shut. Some of my polytunnels were a bit dicey, due to their height.

"Morning, Diana! How are you? What do you think about all this kerfuffle over an election?" Samara greeted me, looking far cheerier than she had when she'd been waiting for me on my doorstep that rainy day. I hoped it meant she'd realised I wasn't out to steal her man.

"Election?" I wasn't exactly up to speed on current affairs.

"Yes, you didn't know? They did only announce it last night. It's a snap election because no one can agree to a darn thing in government at the moment." She shook her head. "I don't know why they expect this to change anything, but it is what it is. Most of the candidates for our district are claiming to live in our locality, but I certainly haven't seen them around. I reckon they all claim that so that you think they're some average village person - someone who's just like you. Really, they spend most of their time up in the city and don't care a jot about we locals - just their political careers."

I found that I didn't disagree with Samara's opinion.

"Still... this year there is an independent running. Do you know Georgina Farley?"

"She was the executor for Jim Holmes' will," I told her, curious as to how Samara knew her.

She nodded. "She's great, isn't she? She helps me with all of the legal stuff that goes along with running *The Kingston Hill Times*. You'd be surprised how many people think they can make a quick buck by suing you these days. She tramples them before they even dare bring it up in court." I found I could certainly imagine that being the case. After all, I hadn't heard a peep from Nina Holmes since the day she'd come round and threatened to take everything from me.

"Good for her," I said, thinking she'd probably do a great job, but wondering at the same time what would become of her law practice. Surely the woman didn't have enough time to run a campaign and potentially work as an MP as well?

As if reading my mind, Samara continued: "She's been doing law for so long that she's decided she wants to do something new. She's using the newspaper designers I employ to do her campaign, and we're lending her our full support," she proudly informed me.

"I'm sure she'll do great." I'd want to know more about what Georgina was standing for, but I thought that out of anyone, she would have a good understanding of the problems in our area and have an idea of how to effectively, and legally, overcome them.

A cloud seemed to pass across Samara's expression. "I'm sure she will. Although... just between us..." She cleared her throat and looked at me. I tried to give her a confidence-filling look back. "Georgina hooked up with Jay years ago. He only came clean to me last night after Georgina called me up and we agreed the campaign. He was really sketchy about the timeline. I think it actually may have been whilst he was still with Kerrie, or maybe soon after she left. He said something about Georgina being married." She bit her lip. "I know it's all in the past, but it hardly fills you with faith in a man's fidelity, does it?"

I shot Samara a sympathetic look, privately knowing that her chosen had a reputation for messing women around. "I think we have to learn how to trust and who to trust," I said diplomatically.

My neighbour nodded, as though I'd actually said something worth listening to. Fortunately, I was saved from any more uncomfortable conversation by the sound of one of the builders shouting in alarm. There was a nasty crunch as Spencer and Francesca's garden wall collapsed into the shrub-covered verge that bordered the lane.

We watched the workmen rush over to inspect the damage, poking about in the high grass and dense weed-growth.

"I hope our new neighbours get a discount..." Samara joked right before the second shout went up.

"There's a skull here!"

10

THE SHOWDOWN OF THE SUMMER

My stomach did a cartwheel. I struggled to keep my composure in front of Samara.

My neighbour turned to me with a frown on her face. "Did they just say they found a skull? Do you think it's some poor animal?"

The builder reached down and picked up the skull in question, raising the yellowing dome up to have a better look at it.

"I don't think so," I supplied as we both looked on.

"Do you think it's real? Surely it's just one of those silly props?" Samara looked genuinely curious. Either she was a world-class actress, or I could eliminate the possibility of her having any knowledge of the skull's identity and the skeleton I was keeping in my attic. I decided there and then that I did not think Samara had murdered her daughter, or been party to her tragic death. She probably genuinely was travelling the world in search of a new drug-free life.

I thought that it was also pretty unlikely that she'd murdered Troy in a case of revenge served cold. She'd made it clear that she wasn't about to mourn his death, but I didn't think she'd suddenly decide to bump-off her daughter's drug supplier after all these years if her daughter was still alive and presumably having a good time out in the wider world.

"Look at this, Mr Briggs!" the builder with the skull said. He lifted it up and clacked its jaw. "Creepy, huh?"

"Put that down, Wayne! It looks like it's real," a man with a handlebar moustache and the start of a beergut chided him, waddling over to the skull-wielding man.

"It is real! How strange is that? Finding a skull by the side of the road? Makes you wonder where the rest of it is..." Wayne said, chattily continuing the conversation. Until the final phrase, I hadn't been willing to give Wayne's intelligence much credence.

I kept my face puzzled in case Samara was looking over at me. I may not believe she was the one who knew about the skeleton, but any strange reaction from me could be passed along as gossip to another neighbour. I was convinced that one of them did know the truth.

"What's going on?"

I looked away from the skull in time to see Francesca Byrne walk round the side of the builder's van. She took in the scene in front of her, her hands protectively covering her pregnant belly. "My wall!"

"Don't worry, Ma'am. We'll repair it for you at no extra cost," Mr Briggs assured her.

"Too right you will! I suppose I should have expected this. This is what you get when you trust a recommendation from a relative." The way she rolled her eyes gave me a big hint as to whom she may be referring.

"We have also just uncovered a skull. I think the police should probably be contacted," Mr Briggs continued.

Francesca looked at the grinning builder holding the equally smiley skull and blinked a couple of times. "Oh. Yes, probably," she said, behaving as if finding a skull wasn't anything out of the ordinary. "It's probably been there since forever."

"Probably," the builder said, ready to agree with his client on anything he could in order to appease her. "Even so, it's best to get these things checked."

Francesca sighed. "Fine. I'll go get Uncle Walter. He must have cleared the biscuit plate by now."

She marched back up the path and shouted something into the house. A moment later Merryfield's detective appeared in the doorway and walked towards the gathered witnesses.

We made unfortunate eye contact.

"What is it? Another murder? You're becoming quite the crime-scene junkie. I've got a mind to arrest you," Walter Miller said, incendiary as always.

I jerked a thumb behind me. "I live here, remember? If I were you, I'd be cautious about threatening to arrest people when you have zero evidence." I raised an eyebrow, knowing I was summoning the memory of his unfortunate arrest of Laura Fray on her wedding day. Although she'd got out in time to enjoy her reception, I was willing to bet it wasn't something she or any of the other guests were going to forget in a hurry. Walter Miller wasn't going to win any future popularity contests.

"What is it? Francesca said something about a skull..." he grumbled, ignoring my comments and turning to face the builders.

Wayne lowered the skull guiltily. "Sorry. Didn't think it was a crime or anything."

"Put it down. There might still be some evidence that will tell us how it got there," Walter Miller said, apparently deciding to behave like a police officer for once. It was too bad he'd picked a crime scene where any evidence had probably disappeared years ago, washed away by the English rainfall. I also had a strong suspicion that this wasn't the actual scene of any crime.

"Whose do you think it is?" Samara whispered to me, her eyes all wide. I'd almost forgotten that she was next to me.

"We'll be doing our best to find that out, Ma'am," Walter Miller said, picking up on her words and moving over to address Samara in a polite and professional way. "We are here to stop crime in all neighbourhoods. You can rest assured we will be devoting our time to this case."

Samara looked nonplussed by the PR speech. "Will you be able to do one of those facial reconstructions like they do in all the TV shows? They're very impressive. With just a skull, they build up a whole face, and then someone recognises them."

I bit the inside of my cheek to keep from laughing at the idea of Walter Miller giving it a shot with a pot of plasticine.

"We will of course try every avenue in order to identify this person and discover if a crime has been committed."

"I'd say it has. It's a freakin' head and no body. Where's the rest of it?" Wayne cut in, still holding the skull.

"Put that down," Walter said, shooting him a glare.

"Have you got any closer to catching that burglar? I know they didn't take anything, but it's unfair that I had to shell out for a new pane of glass for my front door," Samara said, seizing the opportunity.

Walter Miller started to look harried. "There have been quite a few break-ins in this area. We are looking into it and are ready to act, should it happen again."

"You'd better, Uncle Walter! We didn't saddle ourselves with a crippling mortgage so our child can grow up in a crime-filled area," Francesca told him. "I bet we could have got this place cheaper if we'd known someone had been murdered on our doorstep."

"Now, now… no-one's saying it's murder. It could have a

perfectly reasonable explanation, like a medical school faculty member driving by and tossing a skull out of their window," Detective Miller invented.

It was too bad that we lived down a dead-end road and had no medical schools nearby that I knew of.

I raised my eyebrows. "With out-of-the-box thinking like that, it's no wonder you're head of the Merryfield police force."

I hastily nodded goodbye to Samara and Francesca. Then I got in my car and drove away before Walter Miller could figure out if I'd been insulting him or not.

Even with my flowers in peril, I couldn't afford to shirk the business side of my new business. Today I was hitting Kingston Hill before moving onto some of the other local towns in the hopes of striking deals with florists and advertising with events firms. I hoped to come away with some fresh orders that I prayed I'd be able to fulfil. Those raised beds would have to go up fast.

I was onto my second florist after a tentative first order of some chrysanthemums (with potential for it to be more if the first lot were good) when I bumped into Georgina Farley coming down the high-street. She wore a blue and pink rosette and was holding a stack of leaflets. For a second, I was amazed by the speed of which she'd prepared the leaflets and had got them printed, before I remembered she was one of the most efficient women I'd ever met.

"Morning, Diana! I'm running to be the MP for our constituency. Would you like to see my manifesto?" She placed a hand on her stack of leaflets all featuring her not unattractive smiling face. I was pretty sure she'd do well enough just off the back of that.

I was also impressed she'd bothered to memorise my name.

"Of course. I think it's great that you're running. I've no idea how you've found the time?"

She shrugged self-deprecatingly. "You'd be surprised. I've had my fair share of drama during the last couple of years, but now things seem to have gone quiet. I thought a new challenge was just what I needed." She cleared her throat. "A fair amount of my own dirty laundry was aired during that time. There aren't any fresh surprises anyone can dig up on me."

"No skeletons in your closet?" I said with a smile. The smile dropped when I realised the double meaning of my words.

Georgina Farley shot me a sharp look. "No, nothing like that."

We looked at each other for a long moment.

"I should be getting on. I'm off to Gigglesfield after this. Got a whole zoo to canvas!" the lawyer said, carefully avoiding making reference to anything that had gone before.

I got the message loud and clear. Georgina Farley had been given a fairly good idea of just what was lurking on the property she'd handed over to me. However, now she was running to be an MP, she couldn't afford to have her name embroiled with any murder scandals - no matter how old they may be.

I let her walk away and wished her the best in her campaign. Even though I felt that she'd partially set me up, I still found myself liking the tenacious lawyer. She was good at her job and she did what she promised. I hadn't heard from Nina Holmes or her 'lawyer' since I'd passed along the message to Georgina, and aside from the skeleton in the planter, there hadn't been any unforeseen problems.

Apart from the land, I gloomily added as I walked down the street with my order sheets in a folder by my side. I was working hard on my raised beds, but when I'd envisaged having a flower growing business, I certainly hadn't expected everything to be grown that way. For one, it was going to blow my budget out of the water if I needed to purchase that much compost, as opposed to ploughing the land and adding a topping. Secondly, it definitely didn't give me the range of growing options I needed longterm to make the business a success. Not all of the plants I grew would like it in a constrictive raised bed.

I frowned as I approached the next florist, before remembering I needed to put on a positive face for the sake of my business. I took a couple of moments to stand outside and let all of the worries go. No matter what happened in the future, it all relied on me being able to sell my services. I patted my hair into place and thought about how I was doing the very thing I loved most in the world - that always brought a genuine smile to my face. Then, with worries and thoughts about the future firmly shut away, I went in to make my pitch.

***

The day of the summer party rolled around in what felt like no time at all. It was only when Alice and I passed in the lane and she enquired what time I'd be getting there that I actually remembered. For a second, I panicked, wondering how I'd get in contact with Fergus to ask if he was still coming with me. Then, I remembered I had his number on my phone- courtesy of the dog I still wasn't convinced had ended up on my doorstep due to pure coincidence.

One phone call later, I was relieved to find he was still coming. I really did feel that I was over Spencer Byrne and mature enough to spend time with him at the barbecue, but that didn't mean I wanted to be without a date. *Not that this is a date,* I reminded myself. I sighed a little and raised my eyes to the heavens. Fergus was an intelligent man who was pretty nice to look at, too. If he just kept his tin-foil theories to himself, I would probably be the envy of every other woman at the party. Tom edged him, if it was done on looks alone, but Fergus had the interest factor in spades. I shook myself, remembering that this wasn't a proper date. I knew that Fergus had invited himself along mostly so he could get the latest gossip on the wedding murder.

I looked into the mirror and reflected that the last time I'd been so concerned about my appearance had been when I'd made the poor decision to go and watch Spencer get married. I told myself it didn't matter what I looked like. I had nothing to prove and no one to prove it to. But all the same, I felt a certain sense of pride as I looked approvingly at the dark blue lace summer dress, covered in subtle butterfly pattern, that set off my auburn hair. I was in my twenties, and I looked great. I figured I should enjoy it whilst it lasted.

The doorbell rang a few moments later just as I was starting to get cold feet about the whole thing.

I opened it with a smile, expecting to see Fergus on the doorstep. Instead, Spencer looked back at me.

"Can I come in?" he asked. I observed the way his hands were twisting around each other.

"Of course. Is something wrong?" I stepped back to allow him to pass. A glance out of the door behind him told me that he was alone. There was no sign of movement from inside his house. For one chilling moment, I was reminded that there was a killer on the loose in the neighbourhood, but I discounted it as soon as I thought it. Spencer and Francesca had left for their honeymoon the day after their wedding. They'd had no time to be killing Troy Wayland.

"I just thought it was time we had a talk," Spencer began.

Uh-oh, I did not like the sound of that.

"Talk away!" I said, forcing a polite smile.

"I know we had feelings for one another in the past," he said, turning an interesting shade of red. "I know there was almost something between us, too. If it weren't for my gap year..." he shrugged. "What's happened has happened. I just wanted to make sure you're okay. I know it must be hard having us living right across the street from you..."

It was at that moment I realised this wasn't some awkward ironing out of any tension that might have remained between us. Spencer was acting like I was some poor single girl who cried herself to sleep every night just because he'd picked another woman to marry.

I was not okay with that.

"It's no problem at all! I'm going to be selling the house very soon," I announced, surprising myself as well as Spencer.

"You don't have to do that. We can make this fine between us. Francesca doesn't even know..."

"There's nothing for her to know about us. There never really was an 'us'. And I'm not moving away because of that. I'm moving because I don't think this place is going to suit my business after all," I confessed, realising it was a truth I'd been hiding from these past few days.

Jim had given me this property as a gift, but it had come with strings attached. One was the skeleton in the urn, and the other was the soil infested with parasites that I was willing to bet he'd never figured out a way to overcome. It had driven him back to the village. I thought it was probably going to drive me to greener pastures, too.

Spencer nodded with far too much sincerity, clearly not believing the reason I'd just given him. With near perfect timing, the doorbell rang again.

I opened the door and smiled at Fergus. He'd come

dressed in dark blue chinos and a white shirt that was clearly tailored to fit him. Either conspiracy theory investigation paid well, or he simply liked to spend money on his appearance. He extended a hand that contained a small, wrapped package. I took it curiously.

"I figured you probably had enough flowers, so I took the liberty of picking something else to say thanks for the invitation." He winked at me and then seemed to notice Spencer for the first time. "Am I interrupting something?"

"No, not at all. Spencer was just leaving to get Francesca. We'll all meet up again at the party, I'm sure," I said, unable to keep the smug note from my voice.

Spencer was still looking Fergus up and down and drawing all of the conclusions I'd hoped he would. "Sure... see you there, Diana," he said, the pitying expression gone from his face.

I subtly raised my eyebrows at him. He could keep his pity. I was doing just fine.

As Fergus and I watched Spencer walk back down the path that led to the lane, I felt a stab of annoyance that I'd needed Fergus' help to prove it to Spencer. The truth was I was doing perfectly well on my own and I didn't need to be propped up by a man for that to be the case. I didn't want anyone feeling sorry for me - especially when I was mostly having the time of my life.

"Thanks," I said, breaking the comfortable silence that had fallen between us.

"An old friend of yours?" Fergus asked.

"Something like that." I looked down at the wrapped package Fergus claimed to have brought in lieu of flowers.

"I thought so. That's actually a book I think you should read. It is something of an alternative history of the area we live in. I think you'll find it interesting. It even examines some of the reasons that the land here is so bad." He dropped me another wink, clearly thinking our running joke was still in place.

"About that..." I said and came clean about the materialisation of the killer nematodes - unlike anything I'd been able to find evidence of existing.

Fergus' expression grew grave. "I'm sure if you studied them, you'll find they're the normal kind. It's something about this place which is making their behaviour abnormal. The book will tell you more, but it's largely due to minerals in the soil, magnetic fields, and ley lines actually crossing in the middle of your fields. It's what a researcher like me would call a perfect storm."

"Right," I said, still unwilling to throw in with the crazy lot. "The end result is, I'm up a creek without a paddle because my flower business is going to fail. Unless I do something drastic."

Fergus glanced at his wristwatch - an antique looking thing. "The party's starting now, but who the heck wants to be on time for a party? Tell me what your plan is." He sat down on the sofa. Diggory loped over and rested his hairy head on Fergus' legs, probably covering his smart trousers with dog hair. Fergus didn't seem to mind.

I sat down next to him with the dog between us, and then I finally spoke the thoughts that had been running around in my head ever since I'd discovered the cause of my plants' demise. When I'd finished, I looked up at Fergus to see what he was thinking.

His forehead was furrowed. "Just to recap... you're going to do anything and everything you can to last through the summer, whilst putting the house up for sale, with the stipulation that you move out in the winter. In the meantime, you find yourself somewhere else that you'll be able to afford if you can sell this place. You sacrifice the winter's earnings pretty much entirely, but then focus on relaunching early next year in a place where the land definitely won't be deadly to all forms of life." He flashed me a grin. "Don't worry, I'll make sure it doesn't have any dark history or crossing ley lines. No bad vibes, I promise."

"That does seem to cover it," I said, thinking back through all I'd said and the succinct manner in which Fergus had put it all together. "I don't know if it's crazy. I'm praying the raised beds and some last minute planting will get me through the summer. I hope I'll be able to sell enough and that nothing else will go wrong or start dying." I bit my lip knowing I was actually starting to wonder if there was anything to Fergus' nutty theories about the negative impact on the actual neighbourhood. "I hope I'll be able to sell the house and land and that I'll get enough for it in order to be able to get somewhere that also has enough land for this business to work. I'll live in a shed if I have to."

"Really?" For a moment, Fergus looked thoughtful again, before he shook his head and smiled. "You're really committed to this, aren't you?"

I smiled and nodded, feeling my passion for all things floriculture lighting me up. I knew I had a long way to go, both in terms of business and in terms of learning the ropes of flower growing, but there was something inside that told me it was what I was supposed to be doing. This was it. This was what I was made for. I wasn't about to stand by and let it fail. "I'd do just about anything to make Diana Flowers Blooms succeed."

"Would you even... murder someone?" Fergus asked, raising both eyebrows at me.

I stared at him agape for a couple of seconds before realising what he was getting at. "I should have known you wouldn't be able to let my admittance that I worked as a chemist go! I didn't kill Troy Wayland." All the same, I found there was a smile on my face. Fergus was pulling my leg.

"Darn, I thought I'd get a confession for sure. We bonded over your business and everything!"

I shot him what I hoped was an amused, but withering, look. "I'm afraid I'm innocent, but thanks for listening... even with your ulterior motive."

Fergus waved a hand. "Anytime. It's always nice to find someone who loves what they're doing with their life. It's rarer than you might think."

I found I agreed completely with him. Hadn't I already begun to realise that old friends I'd once shared so much in common with now didn't know how to behave around me? There were those who loved their nine to fives, and I respected that, but for most people, I knew it was just a slog to get through the day and then to the end of the week - all to get paid enough to be able to afford to live in order to do it all over again the next week. I didn't have that in common with them any longer. But I did have something in common with Fergus, didn't I? As nonsensical as I believed some of his ideas to be, we both shared a passion.

"We should probably get going," I said, realising that time had flown by.

"Yes. We'll miss all the gossip! Get them drinking and I bet the murderer will reveal themselves in no time at all." Fergus looked delighted by the prospect.

I shook my head. "You're crazy. I for one want to stay as far away from any one who even gives off a hint of murdery-ness."

Fergus raised an eyebrow. "Murdery-ness? I thought you were a scientist. That's not a proper word."

"I'm a floriculturist. We make up new words for plants all the time," I told him primly.

We walked across the lane with the late afternoon sunshine filtering through the leaves on the trees that over-shadowed the road. I took a moment to reflect upon the simple charm of the English countryside whilst also feeling around inside and realising that this wasn't the home I had hoped it would become. I was a woman of logic and reason but even I could accept that sometimes things felt right, and sometimes they didn't. I knew the road I'd just discussed with Fergus was going to be a rocky one, but I also thought it felt like the right one to take.

"Diana! It's lovely to see you," Alice trilled the moment we rounded the corner of their house and walked into the landscaped garden. I could see why my own lawn had been kept in such great condition. Alice and Tom had stunning lawns of their own. The rest of the garden featured a few sparse shrubs, but I couldn't help but notice that most of these little bushes looked like they were struggling, and some were even on their way out. The only thing that prospered was the lawn and the hardy hedge - which mostly consisted of prickles and weeds. For whatever reason, the grass and the plants I'd spent so long getting rid of were the only things that flourished on this land.

"It's great to see you, too," I said, handing over the bottle of wine I'd bought specially for the occasion.

Alice thanked me and popped it on the table with the other alcoholic offerings. "Please feel free to mingle with everyone. This is a 'welcome to the neighbourhood party' as well as a welcome to the summer. Although I hear you might be leaving us soon?" she looked genuinely sorry when she said it. I felt a pang of guilt rush through me and regretted my hasty words to Spencer earlier. What had I expected to happen? Gossip was the lifeblood of our community.

"Well… I am considering it. I was fortunate to inherit this place, but I'm not sure it's suited to flower-growing," I said, doing my best to sound vague.

To my surprise, Alice laughed. "You've got that right! Grass and weeds do just great. The rest of it I usually have to chuck in the bin and start all over again with each year." She shrugged. "It keeps things looking fresh. I guess our soil isn't very nutritious. Most people don't care about that around here. Gardening isn't for everyone. I do hope you'll be careful who you do sell it to though. I'm sure a developer would just love to snap up your land."

I assured her I would do everything I could to make sure that it wouldn't be built all over by some unscrupulous firm. I found it strange that Alice and Tom had noticed that plants didn't exactly tend to prosper but weren't bothered by that. I'd considered being bemused that they hadn't mentioned it to me, but it was likely they weren't aware that there genuinely was a problem with the land. I wasn't sure whether to tell them, or not. I wasn't one hundred percent sure of my own diagnosis.

I also knew I could risk devaluing the property I was attempting to sell. With my conscience whispering that it was unscrupulous and wrong, I decided to keep my mouth shut. I was serious when I'd said I'd do just about anything to make my business work. Sometimes you had to be ruthless.

"Urgh, it's so hot. Why did it have to be a summer baby?" Francesca was saying, mostly to herself, when I walked past carrying the drink I'd just picked up from the refreshments table.

"Would you like to sit down?" I asked, sympathising with the heavily pregnant woman. It didn't look like a lot of fun.

"No. Standing is actually better. If I sit down it feels like everything might just fall straight out, if you know what I mean," Francesca shared. I didn't know - or want to know - what she meant, but I did my best to nod sympathetically.

"Is it coming soon?" I asked.

"It had better be! I can't take much more of this." I privately agreed with Francesca. I'd heard that being pregnant allegedly gave women a healthy glow. Francesca had definitely surpassed that stage. She looked like she'd just hauled a giant rock up a hill in the midday sun.

"How are you doing, sweetie?" Spencer walked over carrying a drink for Francesca. She looked at the lemonade with loathing before eyeing up my cider.

"I feel rubbish. Everything is going wrong for us at the moment. First the builders knock down our wall and mess up what they're actually supposed to be doing. Next they find that beastly skull. And then, can you believe it? We were broken into the night after the builders came! We were both out at birthing class." She turned to me when she said the last bit. "We thought this neighbourhood was nice! But skulls and break-ins are not my idea of nice."

"You were broken-into, too?" Tom asked, walking over to stand with our miserable little group. "I guess that's all of us then."

I supposed I shouldn't be surprised. The searcher must have got desperate enough to take a punt at the new peoples' place - even knowing that the new couple had practically gutted the house. The reappearance of the skull - that I would bet good money belonged to the skeleton that lived in my attic - had probably sparked one final act of desperation.

I wondered what their next move would be.

"...and there's been nothing said about the skull," Francesca was saying.

Tom shook his head. "I suppose there's not much the police can do. What is there to go on? We were broken into, too. I never even noticed until I was treading on shards of glass from a broken window. Alice was working, which was something at least. You never know what someone breaking-in will do if you confront them."

"Spencer... I think I'm going to be sick," Francesca said. Her skin had indeed taken on a greenish hue.

Tom and I left the expectant couple to work things out.

Spencer buzzed off to find Francesca whatever she needed and I found I felt a lot cheerier in my new blue dress, completely able to enjoy the lovely summer's evening.

"Hello all! Thanks for the invitation," a well-spoken voice said. I turned in time to see a well-preserved man in his fifties enter the garden. He was dressed like he were some kind of Lord.

To my horror, my mother was hanging off his arm.

"What are you doing here?" I hissed at her.

She looked at me in equal surprise. "I never thought you'd be attending a party, Diana. It's so unlike you! You're such a homebody."

I wondered if the parasite-infested land could be persuaded to open up and swallow me whole. "It's a neighbourhood get-together. Why are you here?" I said out of the corner of my mouth.

"I met Archie here the other day when I was out in town doing my grocery shopping. He's been staying with these lovely people and is thinking about purchasing property in the area, isn't that nice?" She looked up at Archie with an expression of adoration I'd never thought I'd see on my mother's face. Since my father had upped sticks, and we'd all grown up, she had got back into dating at my sister's cajoling. To my knowledge, it had all been disastrous so far, but it seemed she'd fallen hard for this one.

"Are you staying above the garage?" I asked the man, realising that he must be one of the Airbnb renters I'd been forewarned about.

"I am indeed! Lovely little apartment and the perfect place to discover the region. I've quite fallen in love with it." He made gooey eyes at my mum.

Too much information! my brain screamed.

"Are you here on your own?" my mother said, not meaning it as a question.

I opened my mouth to answer but just then Francesca loudly complained that the baby was kicking her somewhere unmentionable.

My mother leant forwards. "Have you seen the size of that girl you used to go to school with? She just got married the other day, didn't she? Wasn't it to that boy you used to write about in your notebooks? See what you can be saddled with if you're not careful!" She shot me a thoughtful look and I just knew she was thinking 'Although, in your case it might not be a bad idea to get knocked up…'.

"Mum!" was the only reply I could summon up to express my horror at her even saying something like that at a party the couple was present at. "That's ancient history," I muttered.

"Ancient history? Are we talking about roman burial grounds being built on?" Fergus joined our cheerful group with the kind of comment that I'd dreaded him making ever since he'd agreed to come as my faux date.

"Burial grounds?" My mother looked from him to me and then back again. "Is this your date?"

"I think the barbecue might be ready. Let's go and see if we can help Alice and Tom out," I said, addressing Fergus. He looked ready to engage my mum in a conversation that may or may not include references to crop circles and ley lines.

He shot me a look of surprising comprehension. "Excuse us. I'm sure we'll chat later." To my surprise, he gently laid a hand across my shoulders before shooting me an amused look that said 'don't freak out'.

I smiled back at the man, who'd turned from a trespasser to an unexpected friend, and turned away from my mother and her new fling, leaving my mother in shock.

"Did I do the right thing?" Fergus casually asked as we walked over to where Alice was flipping burgers whilst Tom mingled with Laura, Ryan, Samara and Jay. They all had drinks in their hands and Tom passed Ryan a cigarette before everyone laughed at some shared joke.

"Definitely," I assured him, thinking dark thoughts about my mother. Deep down, I knew she thought she was on my side and only wanted me to be happy, but it was at times like this, when she still treated me like a foolish teenager, that I very nearly ended up acting like a foolish teenager. It was a catch-22.

"Burgers are nearly up. The sausages will need a bit longer. Neither of you are vegetarian, are you?" Alice looked more harried than usual.

We shook our heads.

"Good. Because the veggie burgers look less edible than the cardboard packaging they came in. I hope Laura isn't expecting gourmet catering." Alice rolled her eyes a little when she said it.

I grinned having firsthand experience of the newlywed's demanding behaviour. "You've got salad, right?"

Alice smiled and nodded before looking horrified. "Oh, fudge. I put bacon bits in to make the darn thing less bland! I'll have to tell her."

"I wouldn't bother. She had the hog roast at her wedding," Fergus helpfully supplied.

Alice looked gloomily at the veggie burger. "Well, this burger is probably enough to turn anyone back to meat. I'll let her decide if she wants a sausage instead. It'll be a couple of minutes," she repeated with sweat dripping down her forehead from the heat.

We politely drifted away, sensing that the chef didn't want any assistance.

"Hello, Diana." Jay's face crinkled up with a 'do I know you?' look when he saw Fergus.

"Fergus!" Ryan filled in for him, coming over and slapping his stand-in best man on the back. "What the devil are you doing here?" He looked from Fergus to me and then back again. "Oh-hoh! I see. They say weddings are the best place to meet your future partner..."

I silently thought that if you used their wedding as a benchmark, they were a pretty good place to get murdered, too.

As if remembering that very thing, Ryan's face clouded. "Can you believe the police are still bothering our guests with questions? Now they're going after anyone who works in London. As if that would mean they knew Troy! I've told them over and over, Troy was a good man deep down, but he made a lot of mistakes in his life. Mistakes I was willing to overlook, but I reckon they just caught up with him." He looked surprisingly sorry when he said it - in spite of the fact his best-man had been witnessed getting friendly with his new wife the night before their wedding. Even with Ryan shrugging it off as something that wasn't out of the ordinary, I'd have put him at number one on the suspect list and was surprised the police hadn't put pressure on him.

Ryan shot me a sideways look that made me wonder if he'd just followed my thoughts. "We have your invoice, by the way. I'll send the funds over tomorrow. Sorry for the delay, everything has just been so up in the air. I'm not even sure I had a chance to thank you for the wonderful job you did. The flowers were lovely and the cake was amazing! I've no idea how you magicked up something like that, but it tasted fantastic. You should consider a career in baking. Maybe you could be a flower specialist and a baker?" he suggested, quite seriously.

Fergus broke off into a fit of coughing. He knew the secret of my 'baking'.

"Flowers are more than enough for me to handle," I told the newlywed with a smile. Whilst I'd charged a fair price for the work I'd done on the cake, I hadn't revealed how it had come to be to the bride or her groom. I doubted that Laura would be impressed to know that her cake had once been a cobbled together mishmash of supermarket occasion cakes.

I just wanted to get paid and it looked like it may finally be happening. I felt a weight lift from my shoulders. "Thanks. I understand the delay," I assured him, genuinely grateful that Ryan was taking charge. I could imagine Laura shamelessly swanning along with her life, but her husband had always struck me as a decent guy. How he'd ended up with Laura, I had no idea, but their marriage hadn't broken down yet.

"You know, I think we may have another couple in the area getting hitched soon," Ryan said, nodding in the direction of Jay and Samara.

"They're together? Really?" Fergus said, looking as skeptical as I felt inside about *that* relationship.

Ryan nodded eagerly. "Oh, yes. They're the perfect couple! Both single parents. I suppose you know about Jay's fiancée running off and leaving him with Lena when she was so young? He did so well to take care of her. She's such a great kid! I hope mine and Laura's turn out that well when we get around to having some."

"She just ran off and never came back? Has she been heard from since?" Fergus asked, looking more curious about this conversation than he had prior to the disappearance being mentioned. I shot him a sideways look, knowing he'd probably already heard about the appearance of a mystery skull.

"I don't know if I should say anything..." Ryan said, looking surprisingly awkward.

"Oh, go on," Fergus said, knowing full-well that Ryan practically wanted to be persuaded to get something off his chest.

"Kerrie has been in contact with a couple of us. I've been getting letters from her asking how her daughter is doing.

She said she reached out to Samara before me - of all people! I guess she didn't realise Samara would have moved on Jay by then." Ryan shook his head. "It's sad. She doesn't want to contact Jay because of everything that happened between them, but I know she regrets just abandoning Lena like that."

"She only sends letters?" I asked, hoping to establish whether or not Ryan had any proof that these letters were actually from Kerrie. I was only too aware that I had a skeleton in my attic and a killer who might have been trying to establish a false trail, in case their crime was uncovered.

"Yeah, I think it's hard for her to do anything else. It's too emotional, you know?" Ryan said, nodding his head as though this was perfectly plausible.

"Did you ever notice the postmark on the letters?" I enquired. Fergus was shooting me funny looks. I knew I was starting to push my luck.

"London, I think," he said with a shrug.

I silently wondered if Jay had made many trips up to London when he was supposed to be working from home. Wouldn't it be a convenient thing for him to have pretended to first contact Samara - someone Ryan would definitely not be comparing notes about Kerrie with? The idea that Kerrie had contacted one neighbour already would have helped to create a convincing impression that it was really Jay's missing fiancée writing and not a random ruse.

"You're thinking something, aren't you?" Fergus whispered in my ear, looking intrigued. I cursed my open expression and wondered how much I'd unwittingly revealed, and to whom…

I was rescued by Tom tapping on the side of a glass. It promptly shattered and he swore, before laughing it off. "Don't know my own strength…" he said while Alice shot daggers in his direction. "Thank you all for coming to this little gathering today. To those of you who are new, we like to do this every year. It gives us all a chance to catch up on the gossip of the past year from neighbours we may not have seen for a while, and to spare a thought for those who can't be with us anymore." He nodded towards the distant house belonging to Mrs Bellefleur, the elderly woman who no longer ventured out. "And I think we can all be in agreement when I say it's been a heck of a year! Two new additions to our neighbourhood family, a wedding that I'm betting none of us will ever forget…" Laura preened, not picking up on the fact that Tom was most likely referring to the still-unsolved murder "…and now a mysterious skull found lying by our road. I know I write crime books, but this neighbourhood seems to want to write the plot of my next book for me! If any of you have a headless skeleton bricked up in your wall, let me know," he said, winking round at the group.

I nearly choked.

"Stop scaring the guests!" Alice teased, holding out a plate of burgers and sausages. "We're here to eat! I swear I've been digging up all kinds of strange bones in the garden over the years. I thought it was just the foxes, but now I think I might have been gradually disposing of a skeleton! Imagine!" She pulled a horrified face and nervous laughter ensued. I felt my shoulders relax as the conversation moved on and the topic of the skull was forgotten… for now.

The skeleton was something I'd have to deal with before selling the house. Perhaps I could put it back in the planter, pretend I'd only just found it there, and hand the problem over to the police? I'd given the mystery Jim had left me a fair shot, but I wasn't convinced I was any closer to solving it than I had been at the start. I still wasn't sure why Jim had ended up with a skeleton he claimed he hadn't murdered.

For a moment, I entertained the idea that the people who had moved out to make way for Spencer and Francesca were the ones responsible for the skeleton and its now-recovered skull. It would answer the positioning of where the skull was found, and it would also answer why they'd moved away in the first place. Something about that theory, and even the placement of the skull, seemed a little too convenient. It was almost as if that was what the real killer wanted the casual onlooker to think. *And all the while, they lurk in plain sight,* I thought, looking around at the group of partygoers and wondering which of them was a murderer.

The mood lightened after the little speech. All of the alcoholic beverages that had been brought as gifts were soon opened and demolished. I was surprised when the neighbourhood get-together turned into a party that ran on late into the evening. Even though we were an unusual mix of people, when the alcohol flowed, social lubrication was achieved.

"I don't think I can drive," Fergus announced when we were finally walking back down the lane towards my house.

"Don't look at me! I had just as much as you did," I told him with a smile. "You can spend the night on the sofa. No getting any ideas..."

"I'm full of ideas," Fergus informed me, but when I saw him looking up at the bright and starry sky, I somehow knew he wasn't flirting.

I smiled. All these years spent working as a chemist, and I'd never realised I'd lost all of my friends. I'd replaced them with colleagues, but as soon as I'd left I'd realised the truth. Fergus was the first proper friend I'd made in a long time.

I went to sleep that night with a warm and fuzzy feeling that wasn't just due to a slight overindulgence in alcohol.

I woke up at three in the morning stone cold sober. For a

moment I lay still in my bed, wondering why I was suddenly wide awake.

There was a small sound as someone stepped on the slightly creaky floorboard at the top of the stairs. I remembered that I'd allowed Fergus to stay over and relaxed a little, thinking that he was just up and looking for the bathroom. I shut my eyes but then opened them again. I wasn't sure what it was, but Fergus didn't strike me as someone who'd creep around the house, and I was also pretty certain that he was going to sleep through the night without waking. He'd been out like a light when I'd handed him a pillow and blanket.

There was someone else in my house. I was sure of it. I silently cursed, remembering the way I'd tensed up when jokes had been made about the skull's missing skeleton. Someone at the party must have been watching for that very reaction. Now they knew I had the skeleton...

For some reason, I found myself thinking about Troy Wayland's death. My mind was suddenly clear. It was the location and timing of his death that had been bothering me all along. Someone had arranged to meet him prior to the wedding - someone who'd had the wedding in common with him. It had definitely been personal. *But why would he have been meeting with his killer in the first place?* I wondered, and then hit on the most probable truth.

What if Troy's return to Merryfield had somehow allowed him to work out that one of the previous residents we all believed to have left the area was really dead? And then he'd figured out who killed them.

But the cyanide! It wasn't a spur of the moment thing, I thought, before my mind swirled again as I tried to remember who Troy had been in contact with in our neighbourhood when he'd lived locally. He'd supplied Samara's daughter with drugs... and Samara had heavily implied that he'd had an affair with Kerrie. I reckoned Laura could be added to that list, too. The eve of her wedding hadn't been her first encounter with Troy. He'd definitely got around… and he'd left a sea of enemies in his wake. I believed Samara's daughter was alive and well. I wasn't sure about Kerrie's current state of being.

But why meet up with someone I was assuming he'd already known was a killer?

Troy had been in debt. If the police were willing to give credence to the theory that he'd been murdered by someone from the city, tired of waiting for the gambling addict to pay what he owed, he must have been in money trouble. The whole 'killed because of his debt' thing was utter nonsense. No one got anything repaid that way. But that didn't mean he hadn't been in dire need of some fast cash.

He'd been trying to blackmail someone.

Only for them to kill him in a way he'd never seen coming.

Troy would surely only have accepted the offer of a cigarette from another smoker.

Who was smoking at the garden party? I wondered, desperately searching for the answer, even as the killer searched for me.

I held my breath when I heard another creak - this time much closer to my bedroom door. This person had already killed. *And more than once!* I thought, now understanding how it was all tied together.

And I was going to become their next victim… unless I did something fast.

I rolled out of bed and tiptoed round the side, hoping to get behind the door with anything heavy I could get my hands on. I was praying I'd be able to surprise the intruder long enough to get the heck out of the house and get help. At least - that was the plan… right up until I tripped over Diggory lying in the middle of my bedroom floor.

I fell to the ground with a thump. Diggory rolled over and went back to sleep. The footsteps paused and then became louder when the person realised I knew they were here. I saw the door handle turn and seized the nearest object.

The door opened. I pushed myself upright and ran at the shadowy figure in the doorway, armed with my trusty hair straighteners. I swiped blindly and heard them clash with something metal. There was a sharp stinging sensation across my knuckles and I realised I'd just brought hair straighteners to a knife fight. In a panic, I punched blindly with my free hand. There was an 'unk' sound as I made contact with someone's nose. I heard the knife clatter to the floor.

The next few moments were a blur. The person I'd punched threw themselves at me and we rolled around on the floor, each punching and kicking blindly. I took several blows to my ribs before I found myself shoved up against the bed frame with someone choking the life out of me. In desperation, I called for Diggory.

My dog decided to mobilise.

A second later, the grip around my neck loosened as he launched his ferocious attack. Diggory's attack turned out to be a series of friendly licks that merely surprised my assailant, but it was enough for me to attempt to fumble around in the dark. I laid a hand on the fancy trowel I'd bought myself when I'd been contracted for my first ever wedding - only for it to have fallen beneath my bed and remained lost... until this very moment.

I lifted it in the air, unsure of what I was planning to do next.

The light snapped on. I was caught with the trowel raised over my head like a weapon, looking down at a very dishevelled Alice Jenkins.

11

SKELETONS AND SECRETS

"What on earth is going on?" Fergus enquired, looking vaguely puzzled by the scene laid out before him.

"She's a murderer. She's the one who's responsible for that skull the builders found," I announced, knowing it had to be the truth.

Fergus took that in. "Did she kill Troy Wayland, too?"

"I think so. It's all tied together," I said. I'd also realised that Troy's return to town (and probable blackmail attempt) almost certainly coincided with the start of the break-ins. Break-ins I was now sure Alice was responsible for.

"Just hand over the skeleton and we can forget that any of this ever happened," Alice said, keeping her voice light and friendly - in spite of the fact I was certain she'd come here to kill me. Alice was observant. She hadn't expected Fergus to stay the night.

"No you don't!" Fergus said, stomping on the knife she was reaching for.

With a shout of rage, Alice seized the hair straighteners I'd used in my first attack and clouted Fergus around the head with them. Whilst he was clutching his temple, she yanked the large knife free and went to stab the dazed Fergus.

"Don't-you-dare!" I shouted, darting forwards and parrying the blow with my trowel. The knife missed Fergus, but now Alice was back to focusing on me. She smiled and I realised that, not only was I using a trowel against a huge knife, I was also fighting a woman that the bones in my attic would suggest knew how to use the weapon to deadly effect.

"Alice... what are you doing?"

The murderess stopped mid-strike and turned to face the bedroom door.

Tom stood there dressed in his pyjamas with a look of defeat on his face. "This has to stop. It's over," he told her simply. "You shouldn't have gone searching for the skeleton. She'd never have known it was us if you hadn't looked."

"She's not an idiot, Tom. Didn't you hear her asking all of those questions at the barbecue? She was figuring it all out. She knows we killed them."

"I don't want anyone else to die," Tom said, sounding meek. His voice cracked. "I can't take this any more. We've been living a lie for so long. Can't it just be over?"

Alice looked furious for a second. Then she lowered the knife. "Fine. I was just doing it for you."

"I know you were," Tom said with love in his eyes. "But it's time we did the right thing. We both know I'm a mess. I write books about criminals, but I'm pretty terrible at actually being one. It's driven me to the edge of my sanity." He turned to look at me. "I'm the one who killed our tenant, Chrissy. We both killed Kerrie. They were terrible accidents."

I tried not to betray any surprise. I'd expected Tom to confess to the murder of Troy Wayland and one of the potentially missing women - not both of them!

Tom looked defeated. "I was in the kitchen cutting steaks

off a piece of sirloin when Chrissy came in. She'd been behaving inappropriately for a couple of months. We served her the eviction notice because of her behaviour. She ignored it and refused to leave willingly. We couldn't actually take her to court because we hadn't given her fair notice. We should have known that someone as sneaky as her would know the law on that. We were still trying to figure things out when it finally happened. No matter how many times I told her I was happily married, she'd keep trying it on. It was horrible, and we couldn't legally get rid of her. She grabbed me, and I'm afraid I just saw red. When I came to my senses, Chrissy was on the floor, and I was holding a knife covered in blood." He looked horrified by the memory. "We buried her that night in the garden. There was already a nice big hole where Alice was planting that year's shrub border, after the previous lot had died again. I laid down plastic on top of the body, and we made sure we planted things with shallow roots from then on. It was in the dead of night and no one saw. We thought all of our problems were over."

Tom sighed. I realised I hadn't yet heard the whole story.

"Kerrie came looking for Chrissy a day later. It turned out, she'd arranged to meet her at the supermarket because she'd found out about Jay's affair, and they were going to come to some agreement. When Chrissy didn't show up, she came to call on us. We told her our terrible tenant had left town, having robbed us blind, but she didn't believe it. She said there was no way Chrissy would let Jay go 'just like that'. I think the two women were going to figure out who got to keep him." He shook his head. "Chrissy wasn't the kind of girl who had family and friends. We thought we could get away with her disappearing with a plausible cover story like theft, but Kerrie wouldn't shut up about it. She said she was going to go to the police because she thought we were acting all shady. She had to go."

I shut my eyes. "You killed her, too."

Tom nodded. "Getting rid of her car was easy. I have some good criminal contacts - it's a benefit of writing crime novels. You wouldn't believe how many of my fans are actual criminals."

"We didn't think Kerrie would have told anyone about her meeting with Chrissy. When the police looked into Jay's relationship and couldn't find anything to suggest he'd killed her, they decided she'd wanted to disappear of her own free will. Everyone local knew both Jay and Kerrie were messing around behind the other's back. It was almost a comedy at that stage. I think everyone wanted to believe she'd run off to start a life away from that poisonous relationship," Alice continued.

She cleared her throat. "I'll admit, we panicked a little after what happened with Kerrie. There wasn't another convenient spot. Tom just dug up the lawn when we thought it was dark enough outside and put her in the hole. The next day, we laid down turf on top of the obvious digging. But I guess it wasn't dark enough that night, or perhaps the turf was suspicious. It must have been five years later when someone dug up our lawn and stole the skeleton. They left the skull there, like they were mocking us."

She shook her head at the memory. "I thought for sure that I was going to get some kind of blackmail note through the door and have to do whatever it told me to do. That was when I started sending the letters to Ryan from Kerrie. I used to post them on my way to work in London. We thought the city was a big enough place for Kerrie to be hiding. Even if Ryan went to the police, they wouldn't know where to begin looking. In fact, it probably would have helped us. It was all to create the impression that she was still alive, you see? Even if the bones resurfaced, they couldn't possibly be suspected of belonging to Kerrie if Ryan had been receiving letters from her, right? With Kerrie gone, no one else even realised that Chrissy was actually missing. Everyone believed she was just a thief who'd done a runner. We figured we were covering ourselves with those letters." Alice rubbed her eyes. "But the blackmail never came. We lived in fear for a whole year before we figured that whoever had the skeleton was content to sit on it. They must have just wanted to make us sweat."

I nodded. That did sound like the sort of thing Jim would have enjoyed. He'd had a thing about just desserts.

Alice sighed. "Looking back, it must have been the hydrangeas. We couldn't believe it when he planted all of those bushes a couple of metres over our border in the gap that used to exist at the end of our hedge. It wasn't fair. He had three fields, for goodness' sake! We told him to move them, but he refused. In the end, I watered them with the nastiest plant-killing recipe I could find. The bushes turned up their toes. I blamed the fact that nothing seems to grow all that well around here. I thought Jim accepted my excuse, but looking back, the skeleton vanished a month after his plants died. Where was it, by the way?" she asked.

"In one of the terracotta urns."

Alice looked pained. "I should have guessed, I suppose."

I pursed my lips. "I think he wanted me to figure out the truth and then decide what to do with it. I don't know why Jim kept quiet when he saw you burying the body. Perhaps it was because he wasn't fond of Kerrie either." There had been the cat incident and Jim was nothing if not petty. "I don't think he was proud of his revenge in the end. He chose me to inherit because he knew the skeleton wouldn't stay hidden forever... and I think he knew that the local police would never bother to figure out the whole truth." I'd unknowingly been picked by Jim as the person to right all wrongs in Little Larchley. For the first time, I really regretted everything I'd been 'gifted' by my allotment companion. If it weren't for Fergus, I could be dead right now… and it would have been Jim Holmes' fault.

"Why did you kill Troy Wayland?" Fergus asked, as casual as you like.

12

THE FINAL PIECE OF THE PUZZLE

Tom frowned. "We didn't."

"Yes you did. I saw you hand over a cigarette to Ryan at the barbecue. I know Ryan didn't kill his own best-man. He didn't have a motive to do it. Laura's infidelity wasn't exactly headline news, and just between us, the poor guy is kind of a wet lettuce." Fergus stated, surprising me with his observation skills. He'd reached the same conclusion I had. "Only another smoker would be able to give Troy Wayland a poisoned cigarette containing a crystal of cyanide without arousing the slightest bit of suspicion."

"And you already said that a writer like you has the criminal contacts to get hold of exactly what you'd have needed to do it," I observed, wondering how I hadn't seen it before.

"That's not true at all!" Tom protested, looking completely baffled.

"I was the one who killed Troy," Alice confessed. "And those were my cigarettes Tom was handing out yesterday. I didn't have pockets in the dress I was wearing for the party, so I asked him to hold them for me. Ryan must have seen me hand them over to Tom."

"What are you talking about?" Tom said, looking at his wife aghast.

She shot him a desperate look. "Troy came round a couple of days before the wedding when you were out buying stationery. He asked if we had Chrissy's details because he hadn't heard from her for years. According to him, the last place he could trace her to was here. I tried to put him off, saying that scum like that probably just changed her name and started over after robbing us, but Troy acted like he knew something. Then, out of the blue, he said that Ryan had told him all about Kerrie's letters. Apparently, all these years later, he wanted to know if Troy had been the guy who'd persuaded her to abandon Jay and her kid. Troy made out that we'd made some mistake when writing them that immediately let him know it wasn't Kerrie. He said that there were a couple of ways this could go. We paid him, or he went to the police and told them everything... and he'd use the mistake he'd allegedly found in one of the letters to prove it all." She shut her eyes. "Like a sucker, I believed him. Looking back now, I'm almost certain he was making it up about that mistake and guessing about the rest of it. Tom put hardly any detail in those letters in case of that exact issue. The return address was an untraceable P.O.box that I paid random strangers to collect for me. There was no way any of it could come back to haunt us."

I kept a firm grip on my trowel. She was explaining this in an awfully reasonable fashion, but there was definitely something unhinged about this couple.

"I should have known Troy Wayland didn't have a clue. He just wanted money to pay off his debts and thought we were suckers for it. My reaction alone, as he spun his story, was probably enough for him to realise he had us nailed. He definitely suspected something... probably because he'd been carrying on with both women - and I bet Chrissy told him

187

we weren't able to evict her - but he bluffed the rest, and I believed it." She shot a sideways look at me. "I learned a thing or two from him on that day."

It was the same way she'd caught me. I didn't know if she'd actually planned Tom's party speech, or if it had been serendipity, but she'd been hoping the skull and the question of where its skeleton was now would come up in conversation at the party when the alcohol had been flowing. She'd been watching for a reaction.

"I wasn't going to let Troy bleed us dry over something that was all a terrible accident and ancient history. Tom really does have some good contacts because of his books. I used to be alarmed by the criminals who would get in touch with Tom because they liked his writing, but it's been an advantage. One of them supplied me with the crystals without any questions asked, and it was a breeze to put them in a cigarette." She laughed. "It was actually my supplier's idea. Tom could definitely learn a thing or two from some of his fans."

"Why continue the break-ins after you killed the man who was extorting you?" Fergus asked, looking curious.

Alice shut her eyes for a moment. "With hindsight, that was my greatest mistake. Troy had heavily implied that if anything were to happen to him, our little secret would come out. I was paranoid enough to believe he meant he had a copy of this letter with the error that revealed someone was pretending to be Kerrie... and that somehow, it would all lead back to us."

She sighed. "I wasn't thinking straight. We actually got rid of Chrissy's skeleton years ago. There's zero evidence of that left. I figured that if I could get the drop on Troy - even if it was something he'd planned to get us with in the case of his death - by finding the skeleton first, it could all be made to go away. No body - no crime, right? I already knew it was one of our neighbours. It had to be. Who else had a view over the top of our garden? I know no one was around that night, and it's not like our garden is on show. It's round the back of our house. There are a limited number of view points."

She shook her head. "It was stupid. I thought it would be simple. I'd find the skeleton and the nightmare would finally be over - for good. I even broke in to our own house, so that no one would be suspicious. I never even really considered Jim. He argued with people, sure, but his responses were always so petty. I couldn't imagine he'd do something as nuts as stealing a skeleton."

"He must have been far more upset about the hydrangeas than you realised," I commented, actually agreeing with Alice. I also thought that the note Jim had left in the journal hinted that he was ashamed of his actions.

"I think after Troy I just let my paranoia get the best of me. I was lucky that he had a dark enough character that the police assumed it was someone gunning for him over his gambling debts when they found the poison. I guess we should have handed ourselves in years ago. It just didn't seem fair after everything we'd both gone through. After Tom killed Chrissy, and then Kerrie, we held our breath, thinking that someone was bound to come asking. It just goes to show what bad news they both were. No one ever did come look-ing... until Troy." She rubbed a hand across her face. "I couldn't believe it when those builders found the skull after it had sat there in those weeds for years. I ditched it there when we found the skeleton gone and knew that someone could pinpoint where it was buried. Later on, when nothing seemed to have come of the missing skeleton and we were back to thinking straight, we ground up the other buried bones for fertiliser. It was only after Troy came to visit that I thought of the skull. But with our new neighbours having the local police stop by for tea every five minutes, it was too late and too risky to touch it. It's a shame… the garden could have done with another pick-me-up."

I felt something crawl up my spine at her words. I hated to agree with Fergus without any clear scientific basis, but there was definitely something off about this entire neighbourhood - even if it was all caused by the people who lived here.

Alice looked appealingly at Tom. "We could still get out of this."

I tightened my grip on the trowel, reading her words.

Tom shook his head. "We were never real criminals. All these years, it's been one cover-up after the next. We've got to come clean or it will only get worse. Don't you see? The guilt is crippling us both!"

At that moment, blue lights flashed through the windows.

I shot a surprised look at Fergus, wondering if he'd called the police before intervening. He shrugged - subtly enough that I was the only one who saw it.

"The police are already here. It was only a matter of time before they put all of the pieces together with that skull turning up and Troy's death. They must have reconstructed the face and realised it was Kerrie. I hear they can do that these days with modelling clay and computers…" He shook his head in despair. "There's no way out of this now. No more botched cover-ups. We should go out there and come clean. Do ourselves a favour," Tom told his wife.

Alice finally nodded. I wondered if Fergus was holding his breath the way I was. Neither of us had called the police, but for whatever reason, it seemed they were right outside in the lane. Perhaps they'd figured it all out right before I had. Alice's murder of Troy may not have been as perfect as she'd imagined, and the skull could have been reconstructed as Tom believed, but as a scientist, I was all too aware that there was hardly any actual evidence to tie this couple to the crimes they'd committed. And I also happened to know that the 'forensic facial reconstruction' Tom and Samara had now both referred to was in fact more guesswork than actual science at this current moment in time. It was widely accepted to be fairly inaccurate. All we actually had was a confession that the pair of them could later deny had ever happened. The rest was all circumstantial evidence at best. And after all... who was the one keeping the skeleton in her attic?

The couple nodded to one another. Fergus and I stepped aside and let them walk together through the house and out of the front door.

"We'd like to confess to the murders of Troy Wayland, Chrissy Baron, and Kerrie Lawrence... and to breaking and entering," Alice called out to the man just getting out of the police car.

Walter Miller stopped in his tracks, his eyes wide and a vein pulsing in his forehead. "You what now?" he said and then seemed to shake himself. "Did you just confess to murder... murders?" he corrected.

"Yes, we did," Tom said, squeezing Alice's hand, even as she seemed to take a step back, as if finally realising that this wasn't the situation it had initially appeared to be.

I hoped the couple's attack of guilt lasted long enough for them to repeat their confession to someone who could vouch for it.

"Just my luck," the detective said, looking furious. He took his handcuffs out and then turned and rummaged in the car before pulling out a second pair. Walter slapped them on the willing hands of the murder duo. "Alice and Tom Jenkins you are under arrest for the suspected murder of Troy Wayland, Chrissy Baron, and Kerrie Lawrence, and for suspected criminal damage and unlawful entry to the property of.... lots of people," he finished, weakly. "You have the right to remain silent." He mopped his sweating brow, his piggy eyes darting back and forth from the killers to his car. "Now... will you get in the back and keep quiet? My niece is about to give birth, and I do not want her to do it on the upholstery!" He turned his gaze on me, suspicion lancing across his face. "What were they doing in your house? Have you got something to do with all of this madness?"

"They broke in," I said. "I have absolutely no idea what they were looking for, but there was no harm done." I made eye contact with Alice. She slightly inclined her head, knowing I'd just made her a deal. I would keep quiet about her attempted murder of me if she would keep quiet about the fact I'd been holding onto evidence of a murder. I had a feeling that building a case against the couple would prove to be complex, and I'm afraid I wanted to wash my hands of the whole business - even if my testimony could have contributed to an end result. *There'll be evidence enough,* I silently thought, hatching a plan.

"What's taking so long? I'm giving birth here!" Francesca yelled from the front passenger seat and then screamed out in obvious pain.

Walter's piggy eyes widened in panic. He rushed back to his vehicle, probably remembering his precious upholstery. I gave him the benefit of the doubt that he'd forget all about it when his niece or nephew was brought into the world safe and sound - no matter where the birth actually happened.

I just hoped he didn't forget about the murderers in the back seat of his patrol car.

"They've waited long enough for justice. A few more hours will probably make no difference," I said aloud.

Fergus shot me a funny look. "Boy, did we get off lucky with that one. I like my theories, but even I know you've got to have some evidence to make them plausible. The evidence in their trial is going to be tenuous at best. As soon as a lawyer gets his or her hands on them they're going to shut up tighter than a miser's purse. The sudden attack of remorse will probably wear off when they're faced with the prospect of several decades in prison."

I nodded, knowing it was probably true. "That's why when the police investigate their house and garden, they're going to find a skeleton buried beneath the bushes."

I watched the police search from the attic window the next morning. I'd banked on Walter Miller not dispatching anyone until after his hospital run. As soon as the patrol car had left, I'd fetched the bag of bones and removed all fingerprints (there wasn't much I'd been able to do about the doggy teeth-marks). Fergus and I had rushed out and dumped the whole thing underneath the nearly dead shrubs in the Jenkins' garden.

A shout went up.

They'd found bones.

I silently hoped that it would be enough to tip a jury towards reaching the right verdict. I knew that everyone who'd ended up dead had exhibited more than their fair share of flaws, but that didn't mean they didn't deserve justice. And just because no one missed the two dead women, it didn't mean their deaths should be silent forever. Everyone should have to answer for their crimes one day.

I shook my head, wondering what kind of justice would be done. It wouldn't surprise me if there simply wasn't enough to go on. I supposed that Tom's criminal contacts could be traced, but I thought they'd be smoke in the wind if they even got a hint that the police wanted to question them. And then where would the case be? Just a pack of cigarettes of the same brand that Alice smoked, a skeleton buried in their backyard, and letters that probably couldn't be traced back to them - contrary to what Troy had fooled Alice into thinking. The murder weapon had presumably long since been thrown away, and the skull would have been picked clean lying out in the elements.

I just wasn't sure if the bag of bones would be enough. But it would be enough to start people looking - and looking properly - for the two women who'd vanished without anyone particularly noticing. And when all of the avenues had been exhausted, and the only possible conclusion was that they were dead, justice may finally be served.

I found myself flicking through the journals that Jim had left behind. A tab caught my eye. It was labelled 'Hydrangeas'. With a strange sense of certainty, I turned to that page.

There was a second yellow sticky note.

It was Tom and Alice. I saw them in the night and decided it was none of my business. The woman they did it to was destroying that family - although I know her fiancé was no better. I was a coward. When they poisoned my hydrangeas, I made a decision I am still ashamed of to this day. I'm sorry it has become a decision for you to make.

So that's that, I thought, silently realising that the two pieces of the puzzle had been under my nose all along, just waiting to be put together. I turned and watched as the group of digging police gathered around their discovery. What Jim had written about making a decision stayed in my head. I realised I'd already made my own. I'd returned the skeleton to the property of the ones responsible and had washed my hands of the case - for better or worse. Perhaps I was just as guilty as Jim of not answering for my own crimes, but I comforted myself with the knowledge that I wasn't a killer, and the police were closer to the truth than they ever would have been, had Alice not come to kill me.

I'd nearly paid the ultimate price for sticking my nose in

where it didn't belong. I was hopeful that I'd learned some kind of lesson from this terrible mess of murders, but the only thing I could think of was that Diggory could do with learning to tell the difference between friend and foe.

That dog would be the death of me yet.

13

BURYING THE PAST

I t was strange going back to the Merryfield Allotments. I'd picked the end of the day because I knew people usually left in the late afternoon and hurried home for their tea. The evening had also been Jim's preferred time for gardening, and for some reason, that made it feel right. I wasn't so sure he'd approve of Diggory's presence, but Diggory was part of my story. He was family.

I walked the path that had once felt so familiar to me, and I looked at what Jim and my successor had created on our empty allotments. Both were growing vegetables, but Jim's successor was definitely edging out the person who'd followed me. I silently thought it was probably the last few traces of Jim's special soil mix that had made his own veg growing so successful.

"You knew exactly what you were getting me into, you old devil," I said to the vegetable patch, watching as a light breeze shook the leaves of the early courgettes. "But I've decided to forgive you. Even with the suspicious soil and the murderous neighbours, I've managed to start a proper business. It's made me believe that I can do it. I've proved it to myself this summer with my florist orders, my market sales, and my event bookings. Heck - even the flowers themselves are growing wonderfully when I don't let them touch the actual ground. I'm determined to carry on… although I know it's going to mean starting again."

I stood silently for a moment, thinking about all I'd achieved so far and all that was still to come. I'd signed up with ten different florists and four had already placed orders they wanted to be filled every week. I was averaging two enquiries about flowers for events a day and had been frantically taking bookings left, right, and centre. The summer was filling up nicely and so was my bank account.

Despite the suspicious soil and the unruly raised beds, everything was coming up roses. And lupins. And delphiniums. Well… you get the idea.

I left the allotments feeling like I'd somehow made peace with the man who had left me both a blessing and a couple of curses. All in all, I was still grateful to him. He'd caused me a great deal of trouble with his bequest, but the money and property, if I was being realistic, were probably reasonable compensation. I'd have had to turn to extortion myself, if I'd wanted to raise the kind of cash needed to buy a house like Jim's.

Here I was in my late twenties, debt and mortgage free, with a house that I didn't think would be too difficult to shift - in spite of its land troubles. Grass seemed to grow just fine in the nematode-ridden soil, and I thought that Alice had been correct when she'd claimed that most people didn't want to bother with gardening these days. If Fergus was to be believed, there was still some rather dangerous negative energy lurking around the place, but I couldn't afford to feel too guilty about that. Especially when I still believed it was all a load of baloney.

"Show me the science," I said as I walked back out of the

allotments with a hopeful smile on my face. I had a plan to put in action.

"Have you read that book yet?" I looked up and discovered Fergus had fallen into step with me. Barkimedes was at his heels and yapped a friendly hello to Diggory.

"Have you been hanging around Merryfield waiting for me to walk by, or something?"

Fergus and I had chatted about everything that had transpired on the night Alice had come to reclaim the skeleton. We were helping the police in their investigation into the murder and suspected murders. The only thing we'd agreed to stay silent on was the bag of bones that had been in my attic and the part we'd played in their return to Alice and Tom's back garden. Before the police had begun digging for the truth, we'd buried the past.

"Nothing so thrilling. I stopped for a coffee on my way to look at a piece of land. It's just been put up for sale. For the first time in forever, you can walk around and have a good reason for being there. It's supposed to be really close to the site of an ancient burial mound where a roman soldier was buried in a solid gold coffin. It could even be hidden on the land itself. No-one's ever found the coffin or the soldier," he confided.

"I can't say I'm surprised," I answered with a smirk. "I had no idea you were interested in archeology? I thought weird and wonderful was your bag."

I had actually read the book. At the time, I'd found it more amusing than some works of fiction, but it had had the annoying effect of making ridiculous theories pop into my head every time I was close to one of the local sites with an 'alternative history or truth' that was listed in the book. I'd even nearly let one of these crazy theories slip out when I'd gone for a cream tea with my mum and her new beau at one of the oldest hotels in the area. I'd had to stuff a scone in my mouth.

"Ah, well… as for the 'weird and wonderful', the roman soldier was apparently a vampire, and the coffin is lined with lead in order to keep him confined through the ages. They made the coffin out of gold in order to tempt anyone that found it into believing it was a valuable item, only for their greed to be their downfall when a vampire pops out and devours them."

"How poetic," I said, utterly bemused.

Fergus nodded. "It's worth a look. Me? I'd strip the gold from the coffin and leave the lead stuff alone. I'm a smart guy." He tapped his temple with a finger.

I found I was smiling. The thing was, for all of his nutty theories, Fergus was actually smart. I didn't know what had driven him to become so convinced by things I thought were obvious frauds, but his interest intrigued me just as much as his intelligence did.

"Do you fancy coming along for the ride?" He cocked his head and raised an eyebrow.

"Vampire hunting? I think I'll leave that to Buffy."

"Buffy's got nothing on me," Fergus assured me with a grin. "It's a shame though… I would have imagined that a big piece of land, with a house that's definitely a fixer-upper, being sold by a guy who wants to retire to Spain this winter would be of some interest."

I stopped walking and looked at him. "No negative vibes about the land?"

Fergus shrugged. "Just the vampire to watch out for. If you end up buying it and dig ol' Drac up, you'll let me know, won't you?"

"I promise to let you know if I discover anything ancient with two sharp teeth and an irrational fear of garlic lurking around," I said, finding it hard to hide my smile. If what

Fergus had just shared about the land, the house, and the owner was true, it could be the perfect place for my business to blossom.

Fergus pulled a face. "I think that's a more accurate description of my grandad than a vampire."

I gave him an affectionate push. "Don't speak ill of your elders. You never know when they're going to surprise you," I said, thinking of the property I'd been left in the will… and the mystery skeleton that I'd been left along with it.

I'd settle for fewer surprises this time around.

EDIBLE FLOWER GUIDE

Here is a fun little guide to some amazing edible flowers! Please be aware that not every flower is edible, and some can even poison you. Never eat a flower until you are certain of its identification. When buying flowers for eating, it's also important to only consume those grown for that purpose. Supermarket and florist flowers have usually been sprayed with chemicals which make them unfit for human consumption.

Borage (Borago officinalis)

This flower has delicate star-shaped flowers and a pleasant cucumber flavour. They look great as a garnish. If you're a fan of Pimms, you may already have encountered these blooms. Borage can be pink, blue, or white. They're a fun addition to frozen ice cubes for a fancy summer party!

Calendula (Calendula officinalis)

Be aware - only the petals of this plant can be eaten! Calendula has a tangy flavour that is close to citrus. They are great popped into salads. Try them in a lemon butter with fish or chicken! Before eating, make certain you are growing calendula officinalis and not French marigold. Only a few varieties of marigold are actually edible.

Chive Flowers (Allium schoenoprasum)

You've probably already eaten the leaves, but the beautiful purple flowers are also edible. Their onion flavour makes them great in salads and with eggs. Drop them into an omelette for a dash of colour and flavour!

Corn Flower (Centaurea cyanus)

Cornflowers have a spicy and sweet taste, almost like cloves. They flower in pink, blue, purple, red, white, and a dark colour that is almost black. A fun way of using them is to crystallise them with sugar and use to decorate cupcakes.

Dahlia (Dahlia)

Dahlias are relatives of sunflowers and their bright petals look great in salads.

Elderflower (Sambucus)

Elderflowers are probably one of the most famous edible flowers out there. They're often used to make elderflower cordial and champagne. They're a fizzy tasting, frilly garnish for cocktails and desserts. Frying them in batter is also another intriguing way to eat these flowers!

Gladioli (Gladiolus)

With their beautiful colours, these flowers can be stuffed with fillings or eaten as individual petals. They have a lettuce-like flavour.

Honeysuckle (Lonicera)

Perhaps as a child you will have sucked the nectar out of a honeysuckle flower. If not, go out and try it the next time you see one! They have a sweet, fragrant taste that makes them great additions to early summer jams, cakes, and jellies.

Lavender (Lavandula angustifolia)

Lavender flowers have a distinctive flavour. They've been used to make tea throughout the centuries. Lavender goes well with any Provencal herb mix and can be used as a clove substitute in baking.

Nasturtiums (Tropaeolum majus)

The flowers and leaves of this plant have a spicy flavour, and the flowers look fantastic in salads. Great fun for a hot-coloured summer salad!

Rose (Rosa)

Roses are another famous edible flower. Flavours do vary, but a good rule of thumb is that the more scented the flower, the better the taste. Turkish delight, jams, cakes, and crystallisation in sugar are all popular ways to use this versatile flower.

Wild Primroses (Primrose vulgaris)

Primroses have a delicate flavour and make a stunning garnish for spring. Drop them into jelly for an Easter surprise!

BOOKS IN THE SERIES

Gardenias and a Grave Mistake
Delphiniums and Deception
Poinsettias and the Perfect Crime
Peonies and Poison
The Lord Beneath the Lupins

Prequel: The Florist and the Funeral

A REVIEW IS WORTH ITS WEIGHT
IN GOLD!

I really hope you enjoyed reading this story. I was wondering if you could spare a couple of moments to rate and review this book? As an indie author, one of the best ways you can help support my dream of being an author is to leave me a review on your favourite online book store, or even tell your friends.

Reviews help other readers, just like you, to take a chance on a new writer!

Thank you!
Ruby Loren

Fruition

38252028R00129

Printed in Poland
by Amazon Fulfillment
Poland Sp. z o.o., Wrocław